"Clever, funny, exciting and brilliantly readable. A crime novel where the bad guys are our good guys and there are badder bad guys to boo. Perfect."
Gordon McGhie, Grab This Book

"The action comes thick and fast."
Dave Graham, Espresso Coco

"Fast-paced, funny, and fiercely entertaining."
Fergus McNeill, author of 'Eye Contact'

"A deafening and outstanding return to Kilchester!"
Meggy Roussel, Chocolate & Waffles

"Fast paced, full of expertise, funny & action packed."
Sarah Jones, Lost in the Land of Books

"I hardly had time to breathe… Return ticket to Kilchester please!"
Claire Knight, A Knight's Reads

"A fast-paced, entertaining novella that keeps you turning the pages."

Tony Hutchinson, author of 'Be My Girl'

"Plenty of humour, pacey, clever, well-plotted, entertaining characters... My kind of book."

Colman Keane, Col's Criminal Library

KILL IT WITH FIRE

ADAM MAXWELL

THE LOST BOOK EMPORIUM

This book is dedicated with love to my sister Nicola who almost certainly deserves a dedication in a book that's 42% better than I can write.

Tough. You're stuck with me as a brother and this as a dedication.

ONE

IT WAS five minutes before Violet Winters set fire to the Palace.

Apart from that, everything was exactly as you would expect it to be on a Friday night in Kilchester's hottest bar and nightclub. The Tulip Street Gin Palace (or the Palace as it was known to those too cool to call it by its actual name) was absolutely rammed. Outside, velvet rope channelled people into orderly lines. Inside, the walls throbbed with the undulating beats of music so obscure that even the most cutting-edge of the clientele struggled to identify it.

Before it became a bastion of all that middle-aged people thought was wrong with the world, the Palace was called Pzazz. Unfortunately for its owners, it had only attracted the sort of no-budget mid-week student drinkers that were unlikely to line anyone's pockets. As a result, like so many buildings in Kilchester, the beautiful old Victorian facades were either torn away or covered up. The red brickwork was inelegantly hidden behind the glass and chrome shards of what still passed for modern architecture.

Of course, modern drinkers with money to spend didn't want four-shots-for-a-pound at midday on a Tuesday. They wanted one hundred and fifty different kinds of gin and fizzy drinks that came exclusively from reconditioned 1970's Sodastreams. To get served, you first needed to decipher the booze bible and request the right brand of gin. Then you had to wait while the barman adjusted his top-knot, grabbed a bottle of water from the fridge, added flavouring to it, and then shoved it into a yellowing plastic receptacle to give it fizz.

Given the enforced snail's pace of the service, it was astounding that anyone in the place ever managed to get even the slightest bit tipsy, but at midnight on a Friday the place was bedlam.

In amongst the posing pricks and pernicious princesses, a woman staggered forward as if the earth beneath her feet was the floor of a bouncy castle and the other patrons were trying to do backflips all around her. She pushed a lock of black bobbed hair behind her left ear, then stumbled, causing the errant lock to slip loose again and obscure her face. As she tottered off the dance floor, her heel appeared to give way and she twisted three hundred and sixty degrees before snapping her head downward to glare at her shoe. The hand she reached out to steady herself inadvertently landed on a speaker, the bass slithering up her arm and making a valiant attempt at dislodging her fillings. She recoiled and spun around.

A walking homage to 80s cop movies rolled up the

arms of his suit jacket a little further and slid over to the woman. His mouth opened and closed in an expectant fashion. Opened and closed, opened and closed. This close to the source of the aural assault, he could no more hear her than she could hear him, but he ploughed on regardless. She watched for a moment, then bared her teeth at him, hissing like a cat.

In one obviously practised motion, he reached his right hand for her waist and his left hand to cradle the back of her head and pull her closer. It didn't quite work out as intended. Instead of holding her like the wrestler-sex-pest hybrid he clearly was and screaming thunderous clichés into her ears, something unexpected occurred. As his hand touched the back of her neck she slid towards the floor. Perhaps fuelled by the drink, perhaps the unfamiliarity of such towering heels. Whatever the reason, she dropped floorwards.

Somewhere between slipping through his clinch and smacking on the floor, something changed. Her legs, a moment ago jelly, suddenly solidified and she launched herself forward in a majestic attempt to prevent total collapse.

Unluckily for Mr 80s this coincided with her brow being exactly at crotch height. He doubled over as her forehead slammed into his unmentionables, but her momentum carried her forward, pushing him into a full somersault from a standing position to flat on his back, screaming into the unrelenting musical onslaught.

The woman looked left and right, perplexed at having apparently just witnessed someone vanish into thin air, then shrugged and careened away.

Onwards she ploughed, lurching between new lovers and old fights, half-hearted conversations and the spinning madness of the night club lighting until, at last, she reached the door to the ladies toilet.

Pushing at the handle, it gave way too quickly and she fell through, skittering forward and straight into a woman so perfectly-coiffed that her hair remained in a flawless beehive despite being thrust against the wall.

The drunk woman took a step back, blinking in surprise or possibly apology. The beehive gave her a death stare and smoothed down her clothes before resuming her position in front of a bank of perfume bottles, averting her gaze until a third woman emerged from one of the cubicles and went to wash her hands.

"Fragrance, Miss?" asked Beehive with the weariness of someone who despised her life.

"No, thank…"

It was too late. Beehive squirted as the cubicle woman turned, the perfume going straight into her open eyes.

"What are you doing?" cubicle cried. She grabbed a tissue and, dabbing at her streaming eyes, made a sharp exit.

"What are you looking at?" Beehive snapped at the drunk woman, who was still standing, swaying, a look of intense concentration knitting her brow. "It was an accident."

The drunk woman's hand flew to her mouth, her cheeks bulging like those of a jazz-trumpeter. She fell forward and, as she did, a plume of vomit arced from her mouth, showering Beehive from the top of her coiffure, across her red silk dress and down to the tips of her fake Jimmy Choos.

Beehive screamed and retched. She ran to the sink, turning on the tap and splashing frantically at her face and bare arms.

The drunk woman, apparently oblivious, staggered down the row of toilets, her shoulder knocking every stall door open until she reached the last cubicle and fell inside.

Beehive stared at herself in the mirror, picking chunks of *something* from her fringe. Nothing was worth this. Nothing.

They were scum. Drunken scum. If she had her way...

The club's fire alarm interrupted Beehive's train of thought as it screamed like an angry banshee.

"I quit," she said to no-one before walking out of the Palace toilets, never to return.

As the door swung shut behind her, the noise of the alarm choked into silence before returning at a much lower volume, sounding more like a drowning digital duck. The place was falling apart at the seams.

TWO

"BUT I'VE NEVER ACTUALLY BEEN CHARGED with anything."

"More through blind luck than talent." Detective Sergeant Zachary Roach resisted the urge to slam his fist on the table between them.

Lucas Vaughan ran his fingers through his mousy-brown hair and flashed the good detective a grin. "I'm one lucky bastard."

"And yet here you sit," replied Roach.

"And yet here I sit," said Lucas. "Can I have a coffee? It's late."

The detective stared at Lucas. It was late, but who knew when he would get another opportunity to put Vaughan through the ringer? Lucas had been small fry, committing crimes so uninteresting that no-one really gave a shit about him. The word on the street, however, was that he'd moved up in the world. Perhaps even attached himself to a crew. The detective knew he had nothing he could charge Lucas with, but he couldn't let the slippery fucker back on the streets without shaking his tree a little. Or a lot.

"Come on, Lucas," said Roach, laying his hands palm-up on the table and giving his suspect a friendly smile. "I know what you've been up to. You might as well just admit it."

"Why, detective." Lucas fluttered his eyelashes at Roach and pretended to fan himself with his hand. "I'm flattered you're so interested in little old me." He dropped the theatrics and added seriously. "I asked to see you because I want to tell you about…"

"We'll get to that," Roach interrupted. "In good time. But for now you were about to tell me about what went down last month."

"I was?"

"You were."

Lucas shifted in his chair, leaning forward conspiratorially. He took a deep breath. "You're right," he said, allowing his shoulder to droop a little. "I suppose you'd have found out eventually. Was it Jono? Did he tip you off? Bet he did. Becka wouldn't have…" Lucas caught himself and paused.

Roach didn't write anything down. He didn't need to. Just had one of those brains. He remembered stuff. Jono. Becka. Potential members of the crew. If Lucas said nothing else, Roach had something solid to investigate. A starting point. Known associates.

He nodded to Lucas, who looked away.

"Well, I want immunity or whatever the fuck you call it. If I tell you stuff you don't lock me up. Deal?" He looked flustered. This was good.

"We'll see what you tell me and then I'll consider it," was all Roach would say.

"You know how the Prime Minister is going to be doing that conference thing with the Belgian diplomats at that place on the outskirts of Kilchester?" Lucas clasped his hands together and stared at his ever-whitening knuckles.

The Prime Minister? Roach could hardly believe this. The balls on this bloke.

"We… I…" Lucas trailed off.

"Sounds like you can still pull yourself out of the shit, mate," said Roach. "Go on."

Lucas waited a little while and then continued. "Well, we got the plans for where they're staying. And his daughter's room…"

His *daughter*? Roach had known Lucas was ambitious but kidnapping the bloody Prime Minister's daughter was an insane gamble.

"We heard one of her teeth was loose. The front one I think… and so we were going to bust into her room when she was asleep," Lucas flashed his blue eyes at Roach, "and steal her tooth from under the pillow. Then we'd leave her a coin in its place."

Roach stood up and gave his chair a kick.

"We hadn't decided whether to leave a one pound coin or a two pound coin," Lucas grinned. "I need to ask my sister what the going rate is. She's got kids."

Lucas held his hands out, wrists together, shit-eating grin spread across his face.

Roach ran a weary hand over his eyes and scratched at his stubble.

"The tooth fairy?" Roach wasn't going to smile. He wouldn't give Lucas the satisfaction. "That's what you went with?"

"Hey, this is a high pressure situation," said Lucas, lounging back in his chair. "I'm not used to talking to the police, Officer."

"Detective."

"Office detective."

Roach stared blankly at Lucas.

"Someone was talking about coffee before, weren't they?" asked Lucas.

"That was you," said Roach.

Lucas tapped the edge of the table with his index finger. "You're going to want to hear what I've got to say…"

Roach said nothing, just left the interview room.

Lucas' smile dropped from his face. This wasn't supposed to be happening. He wasn't there to retrospectively turn himself in for crimes, real or imagined. He was there to do a job and this Roach character was beginning to irritate him. He heard movement outside the door and pasted a half-smile on his face, adjusted his posture to appear more relaxed, and waited. For a moment no-one came, and then the detective shuffled in backwards, pushing the door open with his foot to avoid spilling the two hot drinks he carried.

He placed the cups on the table, one in front of each of them and then sat, in silence, and glared.

Lucas stared as Roach tore off the end of a sachet

of sugar, poured it into his own cup and stirred with a plastic implement that was neither stick nor spoon.

The waiting continued. And then, for a bit of variety, it continued some more. Lucas cracked first. He peeled the plastic lid from the cardboard mug and peered cautiously inside.

"I wanted a white," he said. What he saw when he looked up sent him into a spiral of panic.

Roach sat wide-eyed, his mouth hanging open a little, his hand frozen mid-stir. After what seemed to Lucas like an eternity, Roach gave a single, long, blink.

"You wanted *white*?" Roach let go of the stirrer and it fell into his cup. Lucas was ninety per cent sure he was going to dive across the table and beat him to death but instead, for now, Roach gestured to his own face. "You wanted *white*?" he asked again.

"Shit, no. That's not what I meant," Lucas babbled, the words tripping over themselves in an effort to tumble from his lips in an explosion of excuses. "I'm not racist. I meant the coffee. White coffee. I didn't mean… It's just, it looked bad and I was trying to—"

Roach smirked. "I knew what you meant."

"Oh, you bastard," replied Lucas without thinking. "I thought I was proper fucked there."

"Well you just racially abused an officer of the law and then questioned his parentage by calling him a 'bastard', so I'd say you've certainly made some questionable choices since coming in here."

Lucas' brow knotted together and a look of actual pain suffused his face. He stared at Roach, waiting for his cue. The detective didn't give him one.

"Black's fine," Lucas muttered.

"Thought it might be," Roach concluded. He'd made Lucas squirm enough on that tack. He relaxed slightly and started a new one. "It all tastes like urine anyway. Could be tea, coffee or hot chocolate in there, and you'd never know the difference."

Lucas gave a half-laugh. "And yet you brought some for yourself."

Roach shrugged. "Had to convince you I wasn't trying to poison you."

Lucas nodded and took a tentative sip of the beverage. It tasted like an otter had pissed in a tea urn and someone had left it to go stale over a prolonged period.

"Is that a… fishy note I detect?" he asked with a grimace.

"Could be," Roach's face cracked into a smile. "There's an investigation underway to determine whether all the milk in this building is just 'rescued' from crime scenes."

"Building a rapport usually work for you?" Lucas dropped his smile and stared Roach down.

"More often than you'd like to think," Roach replied.

The two men eyeballed one another until Lucas broke the tension with that grin again. He picked up the coffee and gave it a sip. "I've had worse," he said. "Now, do you want to dance some more or do you want to talk?"

Roach gave one slow blink. Lucas nodded in reply.

"I was playing poker," said Lucas.

"You like to gamble?"

"You know I do."

"Where were you playing?"

"In Britain's forgotten capital. Kilchester. Here. Doesn't matter. Point is people play, people talk."

"What people? What were their names?"

"Not important," Lucas shrugged.

"Is to me. Adds credibility to your story. Or deflates it. Like a balloon."

"Some serious people. People I didn't want to win too heavily from."

"But you did win?"

Lucas nodded and reached into his pocket. Roach tensed for a moment. This being an interview Lucas wasn't under arrest. Which meant that he hadn't been searched which also meant he could have anything in his pocket and that included a weapon.

Lucas placed a twenty pound note on the table.

"What's that?" asked Roach.

"One of many," replied Lucas, sliding it across the table. "Take it."

Roach glared at him, unsure if Lucas was idiotic enough to try to bribe him or merely stupid enough to think he could be bought for twenty quid. He stared at the note for a moment, realising that there were several low ranking officers he knew who certainly could be bought for such a paltry amount.

"How about this one?" Lucas slid another note across to Roach, lining it up against the first before tapping it meaningfully.

Roach looked at the second note. His eyes darted

back to the first, realising immediately that the serial numbers were the same.

"They're fake."

"Totally," replied Lucas. "You wouldn't know, would you? I mean, if you didn't know you wouldn't know." Lucas frowned. "You know what I mean."

"So you came here to speak to a detective about a couple of forged notes?" Roach sighed. "At this time of night?"

"I'm a concerned citizen."

"I doubt that."

"I'm hurt by that sentiment."

"I doubt that too."

Lucas shrugged.

"You strike me as a man who notices things," said Roach.

Lucas raised his eyebrows and half-nodded.

"But you want me to believe you won a bunch of counterfeit notes and didn't realise. Also you want me to believe that instead of going up against whoever gave you the cash you suddenly had an epiphany and came to me. Specifically me. Asked for by name, no-one else."

"What can I say? I don't like confrontation," Lucas replied. "And, having seen the error of my ways, and as an inveterate gambler, I thought it best to speak to someone with a reputation."

Roach picked up his tea and sipped it. It still tasted like piss.

"Well, I'll have to confiscate the money," said Roach. "And I'll need to charge you for being in possession of counterfeit currency…"

"What?" Lucas nearly dropped his coffee.

Roach shrugged. "I appreciate you bringing the money to my attention and you have my word I'll look in to it." He stood up purposefully.

Lucas melted into his chair a little further and Roach tensed up at the sight of him relaxing.

"I'm a professional gambler, mate," said Lucas. "I can tell with ninety-nine per cent accuracy when someone's bluffing. Note the use of 'professional' and not 'criminal'."

Roach decided not to bother responding to that. He stared at Lucas and waited for him to talk. Sure enough, Lucas needed no encouragement.

"It's all good, anyway," Lucas continued. "There's more. I'm not finished yet. But if you are… off you toddle."

Lucas picked up his coffee and Roach could feel himself getting angry. He sat back down and steepled his fingers. "It's late. I want to go home. Let's assume that I'll get home earlier if I don't charge you."

"Let's."

"And let's also assume that I'm tired of you playing whatever game you're playing. Finally, we'll assume that, to avoid the aforementioned charges, you are going to tell me what you know clearly and concisely. Right now."

Lucas had been watching Roach closely. The whites of his eyes had a red tinge to them. Not so much you'd think it was a medical condition, probably more likely as a result of working too many nights. He had a lean, hungry look about him. It was time to stop pissing about.

"Elias Croft," said Lucas.

"I'm listening," said Roach. He'd known Lucas was moving up in the world but to have it confirmed from his own mouth and to such a high level wasn't something he'd expected.

"He's going to…"

"Burn down his nightclub?" asked Roach.

"What?" Lucas' brow furrowed in confusion. "How did you know?"

In the last couple of weeks, Roach had lost count of how many times Elias Croft was about to burn down his nightclub. Well, that wasn't strictly true, he hadn't lost count. The count was seven. But the point was that it hadn't happened after the first tip-off and it had continued not to happen for the subsequent six. He had no reason to believe anything was about to change.

Elias Croft was certainly a criminal. Hell, he was big enough to buy his way out of almost any charges Roach might throw at him. But he was also heavily invested in his club. All the way to the hilt. So burning down his own house wouldn't serve any purpose that Roach could discern, other than putting himself out of business. Unless it was an insurance job, of course.

"I'm a Detective Sergeant, Mr Vaughan," said Roach, as patronisingly as he was able. "Knowing things is my job and it's a job I'm very good at."

Lucas muttered something underneath his breath.

"Sorry, could you repeat that?" demanded Roach.

"So you know when he's going to do it, yeah?"

"What?" asked Roach impatiently.

"I'll take that as a no," said Lucas. "Tonight. Trust me, there'll be a burning building and his pockets will be stuffed with these." He tapped on the forged notes on the table.

"I don't," Roach stated simply.

"Don't what?" asked Lucas.

"Trust you. In fact—"

There was a knock at the door. Roach drummed his fingers on the table in annoyance. Lucas craned his head around to find out who was interrupting them and saw an older man wearing a thick pair of black-rimmed glasses.

"I thought you'd want to know…" said the man. "the Palace… Elias Croft's place—"

"Yes?" demanded Roach, knowing exactly what was coming.

"It's on fire."

THREE

THE NIGHTCLUB TOILETS were plunged into the soulless darkness of an oubliette. The fire alarms having now completely given up the ghost, all that could be heard was the movement of the drunk woman in the end cubicle. Then the emergency lighting kicked in and bathed the place in an unnatural green light. A minute of silence passed before the woman stepped back out of the cubicle.

It *was* the same woman. Same bobbed hair. Same height. Same build. But she was different.

If there had been anyone there to notice, they would have seen that her outfit had changed. She no longer wore the Friday night short skirt and low top. These had been replaced with an almost ninja-like black trousers and hoody combo. The heels were gone too, replaced by dark sneakers. More than that, if anyone looked closely, they would have seen her whole demeanour shifted. The drunkenness, if indeed that was what it had been, was gone. Evaporated from her system, or perhaps a disguise

ADAM MAXWELL

she had shed. But no-one was left to notice the transformation. And no-one was there to witness her shove the remnants of her previous outfit behind one of the toilets. Which was probably just as well, since that's exactly the sort of thing the police would be looking for later.

The woman walked over to the wash basins and looked at herself in the mirror. Spotting some of the 'vomit' at the corner of her mouth, she turned on the tap and splashed her face with cold water. This woman was not some straggler from a hen night gone awry. This was Violet Winters and she was in attendance at the Tulip Street Gin Palace on business. And part of that business involved burning the place to the ground.

Violet turned around, jumping slightly as the fire alarms kicked back in, their sirens wailing louder than before. Zoe had said that such an old system might be temperamental. She strode purposefully to the door and opened it with cat-like stealth. Peering out into the wider club, she was pleased to find it apparently deserted. Things were progressing exactly as they should. As she hurried through the empty bar and towards the dance floor, Violet scanned the place as best she could. The club's lightshow had synchronised with the ear-splitting howls of the fire alarm, but at first pass the coast seemed clear.

She jogged in the direction of the cloak room. There was movement outside, partygoers eager to get back and resume drinking, so she picked a careful route through the club to remain unseen. She didn't want some over-eager fireman rushing in and gathering her in his arms.

The cloakroom was visible through a rectangular hole cut into the wall. The opening started at waist height and reached around six feet off the ground. Violet vaulted over it and landed in a crouch, listening and waiting. There was nothing to be heard but the wailing of the alarm. Rows of rails hung with all manner of coats and bags, each one neatly tagged with a number. She ignored all of them in favour of a black backpack, lurking malevolently in the far corner. She picked it up and gave it a shake. It clinked with cans of something. Good. No-one had been messing with her stuff.

Violet unzipped the main section of the backpack and pulled out a bandolier. Instead of the bandolier containing bullets, it was filled with what looked at first glance to be large cans of deodorant. She removed one can from its home and plucked the wire safety ring from the top. The safety clip sprang off and Violet stared at it. Katie had shown her what she needed to do, but this was the first time she had actually set one off. With a spurt of fire, the grenade came to life and thick white smoke poured from its base. She lobbed it into the corner of the cloakroom and vaulted out through the window. There was a lot more smoke than she'd expected, which wasn't necessarily a bad thing. It poured out through the small window and into the main area of the club.

That should stop anybody who wasn't wearing a uniform and breathing apparatus from coming in for the moment. Violet jogged to the other side of the club, making her way to an unobtrusive door displaying yellow warning signs. She tried the handle, only to find it locked.

Grinning, she dropped the bandolier and the backpack on the floor and knelt down, unzipping one of the outside pockets of the backpack and extracting a small leather pouch. Violet reverently placed the pouch on the ground, opening it slowly. She glanced at the lock before selecting a lock pick and tension wrench. Holding them with the tips of her fingers, she went to work on the lock. The tool in her right hand was nothing more than a thin piece of metal with a few jagged points in the end. In her left hand was another, this one straight with a right angle bend at the end. With practised precision she worked the lock until, a few moments later, there was a click.

She opened the door to the cupboard and the emergency lighting glinted off the words 'flammable substances'. Violet grabbed two large plastic containers, took a deep lungful of air, and ran into the smoke flooding from the cloakroom.

The whole entrance hall was now filled and the grey of the smoke had acquired an unnatural green tinge from the emergency lighting. It covered her movements as she unscrewed the caps on the two bottles. Picking up the first, she liberally doused the carpets in front of the doors and the sofas around the edges of the room, before leaving a trail of liquid back to the cloakroom and throwing the first bottle through the opening.

She pressed herself against the wall next to the window, finding a spot where the air wasn't entirely polluted with the smoke, and heaved another breath.

She really should have thought about bringing a mask of some description. Still, no time for regrets… onwards and upwards. She grabbed the second bottle and drizzled a trail, zigzagging this way and that, leading all the way to the dance floor, at which point she dropped the almost-empty container and reached into her pocket.

Violet didn't own a lucky lighter. She didn't smoke. But Lucas had given her his Zippo. She flipped open the lid and tried to click her fingers to make the flame jump to life the way they did in the movies. It didn't light. She tried again and again, but the Zippo failed to flame. She glared at it, before carefully using her thumb to turn the wheel. This time a large flame sprang from its top. This she lowered towards an area of carpet she had doused with the accelerant, being especially careful not to burn her fingers as she did so. It caught with a *wumph* and, as she had hoped, wound its way off along the path she had lain.

She waited for a second, staring, entranced by the flames dancing away from her, until she was sure that the fire had caught. No-one, uniformed or otherwise, was getting in or out of the club without a fight.

The smoke from the fire mingled with the smoke lingering from the grenade and caught the back of Violet's throat. She coughed and moved towards the store cupboard once more. Grabbing another of the large plastic containers, she quickly doused the bar and DJ booth before making a miniature pile of the accelerant bottles in the middle of the dance floor, turning the puddle into a pond.

She took a moment, running through the layout she had studied for weeks before. Violet knew she didn't have long before the fire took hold, but she had time to cover her tracks. Picking up her backpack and bandolier she quickly locked the store cupboard. As far as anyone knew, the owner of the club was the only person with the keys and as far as any future fire investigators were concerned, she intended to keep it that way.

The last point on her dance floor agenda were the fire doors. She jogged over to check them and, just as her research had suggested, they were chained shut. Violet shook her head as she gave the doors a rattle to be sure the locks were secure, but the thickness of the chains weren't giving in to anything short of a small tank.

Perfect.

Why Elias Croft needed to chain shut the fire doors remained a minor mystery to Violet. She presumed it was because this was the most vulnerable entry point and he wanted to make it as difficult as possible for any other criminal to break in to his establishment. It did, however, seem a little reckless to keep them locked at peak times with a full club. And besides, there was every chance a stunt like that would invalidate an insurance claim. After all, who knew when the place might suddenly go up in flames?

Violet plucked another smoke grenade from the bandolier, pulled the pin and rolled it towards the fire door. She did this another couple of times, until the whole of the right-hand side of the dance floor was gushing smoke. Then she picked her way past the pile of accelerant bottles, careful not to step in any of the dangerous liquid. Dodging past the end of the bar, she pushed open a door marked 'staff only'. Finally standing in the doorway, Violet reached into her backpack and, after some rummaging around, fished out an old-style book of matches. On the cover, embossed in large, elegant gold letters, was a name. And that name was Elias Croft. Flicking the Zippo once more, she flipped out the cardboard hood of the matchbook, held it for a moment to let it catch and then threw it at the bar. It was more of a symbolic gesture than planting actual concrete evidence of his involvement. In fact, it would probably burn up once the fire took hold but every little clue helped paint a picture.

It caught in an instant, and she stepped through the door just in time, the backdraft from the fire slamming it shut and hitting her in the shoulder.

It was time to go upstairs.

There's an expression up north. 'All fur coat and no knickers.' Violet's grandmother often said this should have been Kilchester's motto, and this was aptly demonstrated in the Palace. Paint peeled from the brick walls illuminated by a single, bare lightbulb. The original parquet floor was smashed through to the floorboards where the bins had been dragged back and forth over them. A second, chained fire door lurked in a corner, this one so unused someone had painted it shut. Tiles from the drop-ceiling that had been installed to disguise the grandeur of what was above were water stained or missing, leaving an inverted chessboard of ghostly voids.

The one piece of grandeur that remained was a wide staircase that stretched upwards, turning to a landing before doubling back on itself above Violet's head. She made a beeline to the recycling bin, which sat alongside its siblings under the stairs. Grabbing the rim, she hefted it forward then dropped to one knee. Dipping once more into her backpack, she pulled out a litre bottle filled with a dark, viscous substance. Crudely constructed electronics with exposed circuit boards and protruding wires covered the bottle. Violet placed it carefully under the stairs, in front of the recycling bin.

As she stalked away there was a buzzing in her pocket. She plucked out her mobile phone as she took the stairs two at a time.

Lucas:

gave roach information. hes on way better be ready. might of got more info than i intended sorry

Violet smirked, taking a moment to pause on the landing. Lucas had played his part. She stood and stared at the peeling paint for a moment. She had time.

That doesn't say much for Roach, she thought. *A drunken parrot with a vocabulary of less than twelve words could get more out of you than you intended.*

She typed a few words but deleted them and instead just went with: *OK.*

Keeping her phone in her hand, she continued to climb the stairs, tapping open an app on her phone. A large, crudely drawn, red circle appeared in the centre of the screen. On it, scrawled in what appeared to be a child's handwriting, were the words 'Do not press this button'.

"We aren't getting in there any time soon." Scarfe appeared at his shoulder, the muttered words somehow managing to float into Roach's ears despite the noise surrounding them. "Any *counterfeit currency…*" he said the words with disdain. "Well, there's going to be nothing rescued from in there, is there?"

"Why don't you knock off early, mate?" Roach turned to face his partner, trying to arrange his features into something resembling sincerity. "I'll hang around, just so we've got a presence."

Scarfe stared at him for longer than he needed to, then walked back to the car, got inside and sat, watching.

Roach turned back to the club. The Tulip Street Gin Palace was well and truly alight now, the flames consuming the whole of the lobby. His eyes were drawn by the chimeric architectural facade, the lumps and bumps and other features he assumed probably had names he didn't know. Sitting alongside it, looking like a Transformer's glass-encrusted dildo, were the offices of Elias Croft.

Roach stared at the office building, torn between the knowledge that Elias was untouchable and the fact that he had a tip-off. If Lucas was telling the truth then this could be an insurance job. There was precious little he was able to do about that for the time being but, there might be counterfeit currency on the premises. The premises for which he didn't have a search warrant, but which were, technically, open to the public. It wasn't much of a stretch to think he might pop his head around the door, maybe to check there was no-one in there. If he happened to see something worth investigating while he was at it, that would just be a happy coincidence, wouldn't it?

He glanced over at his partner. Scarfe's attention was being drawn by three girls whose combined age was less than his. Roach grinned and slipped, unseen, into the reception of the glass monstrosity.

FIVE

ELIAS CROFT SAT in what he described as the penthouse, but everyone else called the 'bell end' of his gleaming glass building. With a smile, he replaced the bakelite receiver on his mock-sixties telephone and smiled. He ran his fat little fingers across the aged paper of the book laid out in front him, before carefully closing it.

The title of the book, 'A Miscellany of Rare Birds and Other Undescribed Animals', had once been embossed upon its cover but now that and the author's name, Tobias Jardine, were all but lost.

The knocking at his office door persisted but he continued to ignore it, as he had done for the past half hour. He placed the book back on its shelf, its size a shade larger than the surrounding uniform modern tomes, leaving it jutting proud of its younger siblings.

The knock-knocking had become more urgent. Elias stood barefoot in front of the bookcase. The deep, deep pile of the carpet he'd had fitted only two weeks earlier was still an undiluted pleasure to walk across. He made fists with his feet, his toes wiggling like overstuffed cocktail sausages. The carpet was one hundred per cent wool and threatened to engulf his feet as he moved them. Money wasn't a huge issue to Elias. After all, if you ran out you could just print more.

He took a deep breath. "If you don't stop knocking on that door right now," he shouted at the closed door, "I will shoot you through it."

The knocking ceased.

Elias smiled and walked over to his desk. By the side were a pair of handmade Italian leather shoes, his socks bunched up inside. He tried to lean over to pick them up but his expansive belly got in the way and he ended up having to contort himself sideways to do it. He dropped into the large leather desk chair, its cushions sighing in protest at the weight. Once the shoes were on he began to compose himself for the call ahead. He took a laptop out of a drawer in the enormous desk then reached into a second and took out a plate.

On the plate was a single sausage. He went to pick it up then, just before his fingers touched it, he pulled back. He would wait. He wasn't sure if he wanted to eat it at all. But if he did, he would wait until later.

Turning his attention back to his laptop, he opened it up and clicked to activate the video messaging.

In an instant he was confronted with a high definition picture cropped just below his own jowly face and reaching just above his full head of too-black hair, a dyed mop of hair plugs battling in the face of male-pattern baldness. He grinned and gave himself a little wink, apparently impressed by the cross between an obese late-era Elvis impersonator and Alfred Hitchcock's reanimated corpse.

Elias paged down through the contacts until he found the one he was looking for.

Felix Thrust.

He glanced at the time in the corner of the screen. Waited for it to tick past one more minute and then clicked to call. It barely rang three times before it was answered by a rangy man in his mid-thirties who looked like he only slept three hours a week.

"Elias," he said. His voice was dry and crackled like tin foil being wrapped around breaking bones. "Right on time."

"Felix," Elias replied. He peeled his smile even wider unveiling a much higher percentage of gum than you would usually encounter in a human.

"Was the vet I put you in touch with useful?" asked Felix. "I never did make a decision about bringing my business into Kilchester." He smiled back at Elias, flashing his golden grill. Every one of Felix's teeth was gold, and his canines were encrusted with what Elias assumed was cubic zirconia but might just as easily be diamond.

"I'm disappointed to hear you have yet to decide," said Elias. "Is London so lucrative?"

"No. That's the fucking problem though. I do fancy me a slice of Kilchester. England's second capital. The jewel of the north, eh?"

Elias nodded. He hated it when southerners talked about Kilchester as if it were some parochial bastion of the backwards. "I'd hoped we would be going into business together. That I'd already be heading up your expansion."

Felix squinted at him from the laptop screen. "An associate of mine has recommended Big Terry."

"Big Terry?" Elias nodded. So this *was* the game. He was prepared. He glanced over to the sausage and smiled. "Well he has a reputation that is the inverse of his stature."

"You what?" asked Felix, screwing his face up in confusion.

Elias knew for a fact that Felix Thrust was public-school educated. And yet here he was affecting a heavy London accent and pretending he didn't know what words meant. This was London criminals for you.

"I mean that everyone knows he's vicious in spite of being a short-arse," said Elias.

"S'right," replied Felix. "But if he's ruthless then maybe he's the one I'm choosing. Maybe…"

"You asked about the vet," said Elias.

Felix lifted his chin, acknowledging the statement, waiting for a continuation.

"Did you know what I needed him for?"

"Nah."

Elias did his horse's grin once more. This was the moment he'd been waiting for.

"I needed him for revenge," he said, a little too loudly.

There was the sound of a can of lager being cracked at Felix's end of the line. "This is gonna be good, innit?"

"I can guarantee it," said Elias, his grin settling down into a smug smirk. "My girlfriend. She liked to shop."

"Women, eh?" said Felix, chugging his can.

"Yes. Exactly. She liked to shop and she liked to screw. The one got her in the mood for the other."

"I wish my bird was that simple," said Felix.

"I noticed that she wasn't going to the usual shops. Every Wednesday evening she was going somewhere else. And she wouldn't tell me where. Avoided the question. Changed the subject."

"Suspicious," said Felix, lounging back on his sofa and lighting a cigarette. "How d'ya notice something like that?"

"I have one of my men follow her all the time," said Elias. "Did you know they have artisanal butchery courses?"

"What the fuck is that?" asked Felix.

"Hipsters go to the butchers. And do a class. They learn how to butcher… say… a pig."

"And you wanted the vet to kill a pig for her? Aw, man, that's the shittest story I've..."

"I'm not done," said Elias. "Not by a long shot."

Felix nodded and waved at him to continue.

"So she'd been going to this place every week for a about a month. At first I think nothing of it and then it becomes clear she isn't mentioning it to me. Usually you can't shut her up about what she's been up to but this… this she doesn't mention.

"I get my man to dig a little and she's the only one at the class and the guy who runs it, he's called Django. Have you ever heard of anyone called Django? Such a bloody hipster name."

"I saw a film called Django. Was good." Felix took a drag on his cigarette and let some of the smoke drift out of his mouth before inhaling it through his nose. Apparently that was all he had to say on the matter.

Elias stared at him for a moment, wondering why he was trying to impress this idiot, and then remembered. The money. The power. The influence.

He smiled and continued. "So I gave her a chance. The next Wednesday came and I asked her where she was going. She said 'shopping'. She was lying."

Felix sucked air through his gold grill.

Elias nodded. "I was sure then that she was screwing him. And something had to be done."

"And that was when you called me."

"Exactly. Because I needed expertise."

"Did you have him neutered? That would be cool. Don't think Big Terry has ever had anyone neutered before. Although I heard this one story where he got two bricks—"

"I didn't have him neutered," Elias interrupted. "Did you know the vet you sent was a vegetarian?"

"How the fuck would I know that?" asked Felix. "I didn't take the bugger out for dinner."

"He took some persuading to do what I wanted him to do."

Felix grinned his golden grin. "Oh yeah?"

"Did you know you can amputate both arms and

both legs from a person and they can still survive?" said Elias, idly clicking around his desktop looking for a file.

Felix spat his lager at the camera in pretend surprise. "You chopped him up? Noice."

"I know people at the hospital here in Kilchester but when I made enquiries… it turns out you need a surgeon to do the chopping and an anaesthetist to put them under. If you want them to survive. Vets are a bit more… talented. They can do both. My problem was that I didn't have immediate access to a veterinarian who was morally flexible enough to carry out my wishes in the tight timescale."

"You are most welcome, my friend," said Felix. He was engrossed in the story and Elias knew it.

"On the Wednesday in question we waited until she left and then we snatched Mr Django. Took him to a secure facility and… He was a talented vet, your man. Amputating from a human is different from animals. He was telling me. Once you've chopped off, say, the arm… you've got to seal off the blood vessels and nerves, there's a whole mess of *stuff* you have to deal with. Warned me that the patient might die. But he didn't."

Felix was wide-eyed and nodding now. "Aw man, that showed him."

"Not really," said Elias, a glint in his eye.

"Not really?" Felix barked an idiotic laugh. "Classic."

"So I took his arms and his legs back to his little shop. And I brought along a man of my own. Very talented butcher by the name of Mister Kelly. And he did some artisanal butchery of his own."

"Aw man, you're a sick fucker!" Felix slapped his sofa and grabbed a fresh cigarette.

"He tells me that the arms and legs weighed about ninety pounds. Give or take. So he takes Django's knives and he slices and dices. Takes out the bones." Elias glanced at a document on his computer where he'd made some notes. "Humerus, radius and ulna."

"Humorous as fuck."

"With the hands, they're the arm bones. Femur, tibia and fibula. They're the legs. By the time he finished we were left with about ten pounds of meat. And so he feeds this into the mincer. Once. Twice... Three times it goes through until he's happy with how smooth it's become, then he starts adding in his secret ingredients. The rusk, his herbs and spices, water and he feeds it into the sausage machine. We ended up with around seventy sausages. Had to use pig's intestines for the sausage casings so they weren't one hundred per cent hipster. But pretty close."

"Aw, man. That's... that's savage," said Felix, slightly awed.

"When she turns up for her liaison the next week he's not there. Was still recovering. Week later and he's ready for solids. So we bring him a lovely sausage sandwich. Brown sauce."

Felix's mouth hung open in a deliberate and exaggerated display of shock. "Brown sauce," he repeated.

"He ate it up."

"Awww!" Felix kicked at whatever piece of furniture his laptop was balanced on and it crashed to the floor.

Elias waited while he picked it up and put it back in place.

"Then I decided to make my girlfriend a meal. Bangers and mash. Turns out she has quite the appetite for Mr Kelly's speciality sausages. Of course I made sure I steered clear of them but she ate up a dozen of them over the next few days."

"Did you tell her?" asked Felix in hushed, urgent tones.

Elias nodded.

"In a manner of speaking. I showed her these," he said and clicked a button.

Four images appeared on the screen. One of the amputation in progress. Another of the limbs being butchered. A third of them being fed into the sausage machine and the last was Django. Sans arms. Sans legs.

"That is… aw I think I'm gonna chuck."

Elias smiled. "She didn't react well. I accused her of the affair, she denied it. Apparently she had signed up for this 'sausage wrangler' course to make me a birthday present. That was all I managed to get out of her before she shut down."

"Shut down?"

"Yes, the doctors said she had some sort of psychotic break. She's completely catatonic. These things happen."

"And she ain't gonna wrangle no-one else's sausage any time soon."

"Certainly not."

"Aw, you're a maniac. I like you. Fuck Big Terry, we

are going to do business. Consider this deal done my friend."

"I'm glad to hear that," said Elias.

"Listen," said Felix, leaning in to the laptop. "I gotta go but we'll meet. I'll come up next week, right?"

"I look forward to it Mr Thrust," said Elias. He cut the call and closed the laptop before reaching over to the plate and taking the sausage between his thumb and forefinger. He examined it closely before finally taking one, large bite.

Not bad at all, he thought. *Mr Kelly is indeed an artist.*

And then, his success, his happiness, his moment of triumph was ruined by the infernal hammering on his office door once more. He returned the plate and laptop to the drawer before storming over and throwing it open.

"What the shitting hell do you want?" He literally spat the words, leaving speckles of saliva on the two men who stood beyond. The pair of them wore identical black suits with identical shoulder-strap gun-bulges and identical unable-to-process-complex-information expressions on their faces.

"Sir…" The man on the left began, but suffered a serious vocabulatory collapse in the face of his irate boss.

"What?"

"Well, sir…" The other man's voice was almost comically deep, perhaps resonating in the void between his ears.

Elias' face reddened, filling with blood from the tip of his chubby chin to the gaps in his hair plugs.

"WHAT?"

"The P-Palace is on fire, sir," the man on the left stammered.

The colour drained from Elias' face.

"Who would dare to do that?" he hissed.

SIX

VIOLET BOUNDED up the staircase towards the manager's office. Flames licked the bottom of the stairs, rapidly consuming her only escape route. There was every chance he would still be there. Given who he worked for, it was unlikely he would abandon his post at the sound of an alarm. More worryingly, there was an outside possibility he might have caught sight of what she had been up to on the club's security cameras and… prepared himself.

Reaching the final landing, Violet paused. There was a small porthole window in the door, a thin mesh of metal running almost invisibly through it to reinforce it in the event of a fire. She peered through to the corridor beyond. It was empty, so she pushed the door open and slipped through.

This corridor ran almost the full length of the building, with a few doors coming off at points and a stack of old plastic chairs at the far end. Violet crept towards a windowless door with a chipped, green plastic sign that read 'Manager'. She heard nothing coming from the office. In fact, she could hear nothing but her own panting, out of breath from climbing the stairs and inhaling smoke from the fire. Still, she waited, her face pressed against the door.

When she was sure there was nothing to hear, she reached for the heavy handle.

It wouldn't budge, even when she leaned her full weight against it.

Of course it wouldn't, she thought. *Because that would save time.*

Violet dropped to one knee and slid the backpack from her shoulder, quickly availing herself of the lock picks she needed. It was a mortice lock. 'Insurance approved' was how they were invariably advertised. She smirked at the thought. If there was any evidence of what she was about to do left after the fire then it wouldn't be approved much longer.

Mortice locks weren't as delicate as, say, padlocks and required a tension tool that was much more weighty. This one even had a small handle like a manual corkscrew. Violet gripped it and slid it into the lock, getting a feel for the amount of pressure she needed to use. With her other hand she took out a curtain pick, which was much longer and thinner, hooking at a right angle at its end. She fed it into the lock, giving it a few half-turns before following up with a twist of the tension wrench and with a *clunk* the lock gave up and opened.

She stood up and wiped the sweat from her brow on her sleeve then pushed open the door and entered the cluttered office. There were boxes piled high on top of one another with the names of different gins stamped on the side. Tanqueray, Hendricks, Bathtub, Edinburgh, Valentine Liberator… Violet recognised some of them, but others were lost on her.

Closing the door, she moved silently to the manager's desk. Stacked on it haphazardly were four slim monitors, each one showing a different scene from inside the club.

On one, she could see smoke billowing across the dance floor. On another, flames licked towards the lens. The third showed two firefighters in breathing apparatus and protective clothing trying to ascend the stairs Violet had so successfully set alight. The fourth screen showed the door to the manager's office she stood in. A stocky fifth monitor sat to one side, keyboard and mouse in front of it.

Violet pulled her mobile from her jacket pocket and tapped 'Zoe' in her contacts. As it rang, she nudged the mouse and the monitor flickered to life.

"Rio Pizza. You dial, we deliver."

Violet froze, moving the phone screen into view to check she hadn't misdialled.

"Every bloody time," she said.

Zoe laughed. "Sorry. It's too much to resist. Everything going to plan?"

"Probably. Looks like it. Maybe. Yes."

"I'll pick one of those answers and run with it. You at the office?" asked Zoe.

"Yeah. Looks like the security set up is as you expected," said Violet.

"Shit, you mean?"

Violet laughed her staccato laugh. "Yeah, proper shit." She was interrupted as her phone vibrated.

Moving it into view again the screen blinked at her:

10% Battery Remaining

Activate Low Power Mode?

Violet's brow crumpled into a frown and she tapped 'No', mainly to get rid of the message, but was immediately distracted by movement on the CCTV monitors in front of her. The fact that she was running out of batteries was worrying, but slightly more worrying was what she had spotted on the fourth monitor, the one which showed the door to the manager's office. The same door she currently had her back to.

Not that the door particularly worried her. What was worrying was that the manager was now standing outside, key outstretched. Violet's eye twitched with irritation as she heard the manager's key rattling clumsily in the lock. Ignoring the noise, Violet continued her conversation with Zoe.

"Everything okay?" asked Zoe cautiously.

"Yeah, it's fine," said Violet, returning her attention to the computer. "Manager is incoming but you'll be able to see that yourself if we get this sorted."

"Are you sure about this?" asked Zoe.

"About what?"

"The job. The job we're pulling right now," said Zoe.

"Of course," said Violet. "Why wouldn't I be?"

"It just seems a long way to go to teach someone a lesson is all."

Violet took a moment before she responded. "It's necessary."

"But—"

"We don't have time for this, Zoe," said Violet. "We're criminals. And we're women. Well, most of us are. The ones who matter."

Zoe laughed.

"I'm not claiming to be a fucking suffragette or anything but do you think he would have paid a man with counterfeit notes?" asked Violet.

"Probably not," Zoe admitted.

"We are dealing with vicious, sociopathic bastards. Getting paid with toy money is the thin end of the wedge. What if next time they let us do the job and just shoot us in the face as payment?"

"Well—"

"Well nothing," said Violet. "Reputation is everything. And once we're done here no-one will try this shit again."

"But the fire, isn't it a bit excessive?" asked Zoe. "Not to mention dangerous."

"We need to take everything away from him. Otherwise he'll just bribe his way out and we'll wind up having to do something bigger and stupider. And frankly I can't be arsed."

"Right," Zoe replied. "Stop pissing about then. Open a browser."

"Wh—" Violet began.

"Any. Makes no difference. A Microsoft one. They're the worst." Zoe waited a beat then continued. "Now type this into the address bar…"

Violet did as Zoe instructed. A website appeared on the screen at the same moment the manager of the club walked back into his office.

The manager was in his early 50s but dressed like a man half his age. For a moment he stood still, as if unable to believe that Violet had materialised out of thin air, but he quickly came to his senses.

"Oi! Mate!" the manager shouted, striding forward and pulling at Violet's shoulder. She moved slightly, shrugging off his hand, and as she did something dawned on him. This wasn't a man alone in his office, bent over his desk. It was a woman.

"Hello, my dear," he backtracked. "I thought you were… well, never mind. Now that I know you're…" His eyes dropped to admire Violet's arse. "I don't know how you got your pretty little self in here but auditions for strippers were yesterday."

This time, Violet's eyes were twitch free as she stared intently, her attention focussed on the progress of the firefighters on the security monitor. They had successfully made it through her fiery attempts to discourage them and had split up. One of them was exploring the floor beneath the office, while the other continued upstairs.

"Do you have what you need?" Violet asked.

"Well, that all depends," the manager replied.

"Yeah, I'm in," Zoe also replied. "It'll take a minute to get the Trojan installed on their system then a couple more to get up in their shit. Then I'll have splice in the footage of Elias going in and out at the appropriate times. Cover my tracks and push it to the cloud."

"Bottom line?" asked Violet.

"Bottom line is three minutes and you never existed on their cameras. Four minutes and Elias is going to look like he set the fire. Five and their system is toast."

"Bottom line is," said the manager as his eyes slid greasily over every inch of Violet's body, "that if you show me your assets and... willingness to please your potential employer then I'll consider a position for you. Of course, you have to appreciate the level of filth these girls were prepared to stoop to with me. There was one, she couldn't have been more than seventeen—"

"You've got three minutes," said Violet.

"Affirmative," said Zoe and hung up.

"Three minutes, eh?" the manager growled in what he probably imagined was an alluring manner, and pressed his crotch against her. "Time to show me what you got?"

With one swift movement, Violet swept everything that lay on top of the desk, pens, paper, even wrapped rolls of pound coins and silver change, clattering onto the floor. She removed her backpack and bandolier, placing them carefully on the desk in front of her, and unzipped the bag.

As the manager leaned forward to breathe into Violet's ear, he glimpsed what was in the backpack. It was filled with money. Wads and wads and wads of the stuff, all neatly tied up with bands.

"But..." he began. "Where did all that come from?"

Violet remained unresponsive to him. Her gaze still flickered between the computer and the movement on the monitors. One firefighter was almost at the manager's office now. She could smell stale alcohol and sexual failure.

"Listen, Philip Gary Gibson of 16 The Elms…" Violet finally turned to face him, then prodded the manager in the shoulder with her index finger. He took half a step backwards in disbelief at what he'd just heard.

"How did you—"

"Do you think that little Janeece Jo Gibson wants to hear what her father really got up to on her seventeenth birthday?" asked Violet.

As if queued up by some unseen hand the computer speakers crackled to life and Philip Gary Gibson of 16 The Elms' voice suddenly filled the room. "…the level of filth these girls were prepared to stoop to with me. There was one, she couldn't have been more than seventeen—"

For a moment the manager said nothing, just stood, frozen, his anger forming around him faster even than the smoke spiralling in the stairwell.

And then he appeared to decide. And unfortunately for him that decision was to deal with the interloper in his office by force.

His hand rose, his fingers spreading to grab the hair at the back of her head, but he stopped abruptly as a firefighter arrived, fire axe in hand, filling the whole of the doorframe and having to duck to fit the helmet through the jamb.

The manager spun around, momentarily smoothing down the imaginary creases in his expensive suit as he took in the enormity of the figure.

"Hey bud," he said, a grin slithering across his face. "I know there's a fire and what have you but I'm sure you could give me five minutes with my lady friend here? I'd make it worth your while." His hand slipped into his pocket and he pulled out his wallet before peeling off a couple of fifty pound notes. "I've got a problem we need to resolve and it's pretty urgent. Whadya say?"

The firefighter seemed to expand still further. Their full height apparently unachieved until now, they towered above the manager and cocked their head to one side. Under the layers of uniform he could see muscles flexing, moving around one another like supertankers parallel parking and causing the head of the axe to bob worryingly. Through the mask and breathing apparatus it was impossible to tell what outcome was being considered, but when the manager pulled a third fifty pound note out a decision seemed to have been reached. The firefighter reached up and carefully took off the helmet, turning it on its side before slamming it into the manager's face. The manager's nose exploded in a burst of blood, popping like a tomato under the heel of a dominatrix. It gushed viscous red across the yellow peak of the helmet as the force of the blow threw him across the small room. He hit the wall and slid down like a rag doll shot from a cannon.

"Katie," said Violet.

Katie took off her mask and shook her head, freeing a pony tail that had been tucked into her collar.

"You took your time," added Violet, a wicked grin playing across her lips.

Katie, as was her wont, said nothing but smiled back warmly.

"Suppose you want to know how it's all going?" asked Violet.

Katie curled her lip and shrugged slightly.

"It's going really well, actually," Violet said, a little deflated. "Five by five. Anyway…" She gestured toward the CCTV monitors. The other firefighter was climbing the stairs behind them. "Company," was all she said before walking across the room to a filing cabinet. She dragged it away from the wall then slid herself down by its side and out of sight.

Katie shrugged and replaced the mask and blood-stained helmet. She scooped up the manager in what could only be described as a fireman's lift. The second firefighter arrived at the door and Katie handed off her unconscious cargo before making some sort of gesture to indicate they should transport him to get medical attention while the search for anyone trapped up here continued. The second firefighter nodded in agreement, before descending the stairs with the manager slung over his shoulders.

As quickly as Violet heard the footsteps receding, she stepped from her concealment. She plucked the last smoke grenade from her bandolier and set it off just outside the door to the office, before closing it behind her. Things were about to get even more messy and that was just the way she wanted it.

SEVEN

DETECTIVE ROACH HAD no idea why he was acting
furtively — he was the bloody police. But he knew only
too well that, in Kilchester, 'I Am The Law' sometimes
wasn't enough. The glass doors of Elias Croft's office
building slid open and Roach stepped onto the white
marble floor of the unnecessarily air-conditioned
reception. The north of England needed air
conditioning like an alcoholic penguin needed ice for his
gin and tonic. Roach suppressed a shiver and increased
the length of his stride, hoping that by the time he had
reached the receptionist's desk he would feel more
confident.

He didn't.

But the good news was, it wasn't necessary. There
was a swivel chair, sumptuous and, more importantly,
empty behind the dark marble of the desk. At last he
would catch a break.

Roach made his way across the expanse of the
entrance hall, quickly drinking in the details, the

potential for interruptions. They were mercifully few. A plain door immediately behind the reception desk, a corridor to the left signposted 'toilets' and another to the right leading to some ground-floor offices. Better yet, before you reached the corridor to the offices were four very conspicuous doors. The doors to the lifts.

The lifts that led to Elias Croft.

He stood for a moment, surveying the scene. As far as he could see there were only two cameras and they were both pointing at the desk. Odd in some ways, perfectly reasonable in others. You'd expect someone like Elias Croft would want to see exactly who was to-ing and fro-ing in his building. But you'd also expect that those people wouldn't want anything more than the backs of their heads appearing on any recordings. Doubtless he'd be able to deal with whoever it was, friend or foe, regardless. With violence, if necessary. No-one would dare to come in here uninvited. Well, almost no-one.

He sauntered behind the desk. Hidden from view was an under-desk with a laptop, sudoku book and a clipboard. If his life in law enforcement had taught him anything it was that clipboards were a source of endless tidbits of seemingly innocuous information.

As it turned out, the only piece of information on there this evening was the staff roster for reception. Roach ran his finger over it and found that the person who had deserted their post was 'Val Morris'. Once he was sure good old Val wasn't about to burst from an unseen portal, he glanced over his shoulder one last time and strode with actual confidence to the lifts.

Four polished gold doors. He smiled at his reflection, his teeth gilded by the gaudy garnish, and reached out a finger to press the call button.

And found that there wasn't one.

He spun around and checked the lifts behind him only to find the same problem. His eyes darted up, looking for technology, a sensor perhaps, to automatically call the lifts, but there was nothing to be found. Nothing except a raised black plastic receptacle with space enough to slide a pass card through. Next to it was a red light. It was unlikely to turn green from the force of his will alone.

"Do you have an appointment?" The words floated with the same menace and contempt they had elicited since they were first conjured by three witches on the Scottish moors in the olden times.

So there was a receptionist on duty. Even at this time of night. Of course there was, after all what self-respecting gangster left the front desk unattended? Roach raised his eyebrow at his reflection, his confidence undimmed by the querulous question, and turned to face his inquisitor.

"Because I'll call the police." The receptionist addressing him was a dumpy woman who looked like she was made of teeth and impatience. She had half-moon spectacles that hung on a chain around her neck, but the look on her face said she was more likely to throttle you with the chain than use the glasses to read a book. Roach walked calmly over to her, placed his hands flat on the cold marble of her desk and smiled.

"There are other people I can call who will make

you wish I'd phoned the police," she concluded and raised an eyebrow expectantly. Apparently Roach was supposed to kowtow to these miniature threats but it just made him want to push back.

"Valerie Morris." Roach reached into his jacket and produced his warrant card. He opened it and, with a grin, brandished it to the receptionist. "I am arresting you for section five; threatening words and behaviour."

"Whuh-what?" she stammered.

"I know I don't look very frightened but deep down inside I'm having a little cry," said Roach and pulled a sad face. "I am also arresting you for suspicion of participating in the activities of an organised crime group, conspiracy to pass counterfeit notes and conspiracy to murder." He really didn't understand where that last one had come from but had no doubt she had seen the aftermath or cleanup of something along those lines.

And at that, he had her.

No matter how many times he arrested someone, Roach never tired of the myriad reactions he encountered. Each one made a nuanced statement about the guilt or innocence of the suspect in question.

Of course the guilt or otherwise of Miss (he was pretty sure she was a Miss) Morris was not in question. On the one hand she worked for Croft, so she knew the score. On the other hand, if she didn't do as she was instructed he'd kill her and bury her in her own back garden with a suicide note on the dining room table. Croft wasn't the greatest criminal mastermind but he was a vicious bastard and he had money.

Roach figured that if he leaned on her she'd get him upstairs. She could pretend... well, she could pretend whatever the fuck she liked had happened to save her arse but right now he had some pretending of his own to do. It wasn't, strictly speaking, legal but in a town like this sometimes rules had to be bent in order to get results.

For the greater good, you might say.

"You do not have to say anything," Roach continued. "But it may harm your defence if you do not mention when questioned something which you later rely on in court."

"No," she said, shaking her head. A frown clouded her brow as she stared at his credentials. This was real. This was happening.

Roach took his handcuffs from his pocket, thankful that he'd bothered to pick them up, and walked behind Miss Morris. He took her left forearm and guided it behind her back, snapping one half of the cuff closed on her wrist. He paused to let her feel the cold of the metal against her skin before continuing. "Anything you do say may be given in evidence. Do you understand?"

The woman gave a half-hearted twist, as if she might have been thinking of extricating herself, but Roach knew it was just a reaction to an unfamiliar situation rather than an actual escape attempt.

"Yes," she said, the fight drained out of her. "No. I mean... Do I get a phonecall? I want to call upstairs."

"I don't think so, Valerie. Do you mind if I call you Valerie or would you prefer Val?" Roach snapped the other side of the cuffs closed.

She shook her head at nothing in particular. "You can call me Val," she said, her voice dry and hopeless. "It was just a job."

Roach was about to launch into a negotiation with the woman, her providing him with the access he needed in exchange for not being arrested, when his attention was drawn by the noise of the revellers in the street suddenly increasing in volume. He twisted his head to see the doors to the outside world sliding open.

In a way he expected his partner to sail through and issue him with a stern rebuke for arresting anyone in the building. In a way that would have been better than what actually greeted him.

Judging by his attire, he was a paramedic. A fellow member of the emergency services and, as such, someone whose testimony would be held in enough esteem to warrant potential career-ending disciplinary action should news of Roach's little charade ever get back to his superiors. He often mused that his skills at getting the information they required from whoever had it was one of the only reasons they kept him around but even that usefulness would have its limits.

"Paedo is she?" the paramedic said in tones that were far more cheery than they had any right to be.

For a split second this wrong-footed Roach. He anticipated a comment, of course, but this was… unexpected. He turned and gave the medic a half-smile of acknowledgement. "Not quite, no."

"I hate to be all 'haven't you got better things to be doing with your time' but…" the paramedic gestured at the crowds with one hand and slapped his shaved head with the other in a weird mix of medicinal and vaudevillian. "The circus has come to town and the ringmaster is smashed out of his gourd on the bearded lady's moonshine."

Roach shrugged. "Uniform can deal."

"None of my business anyway. Don't suppose you've got any first aid kits in here," he said, dropping back into a moderately professional tone before elevating to pub raconteur once more. "We're running low. Not that there's anyone with burns out there yet, but these dumb, drunken meat-sacks are so stupid they keep tripping over the fucking kerbs."

Roach stifled a grin.

"If they're the future of this great nation I might well move to fucking France," the paramedic added. "Is it behind the desk there with you?"

He walked around the side of the wide desk. The receptionist responded as if he'd shoved a cattle prod in her ear, rising on to her tiptoes and making a high pitch squawking noise.

"You-you-you c-cannot come back here uninvited!" she spluttered. "No-one else back here. I… There'll be trouble." She glanced at Roach. "Not from me, you understand."

The paramedic stared at her as if she'd just taken a shit on his lunch.

"I'm not a vampire, missus. And anyway I think that's houses not desks cos—"

"Tell him where you keep the medicine," said Roach. "Be community minded. It'll help your case."

She nodded towards the door behind her desk and

with a cheery "Much obliged, ma'am," the paramedic wandered into the store cupboard.

The moment he heard the door click closed Roach spoke, and spoke fast.

"You have the time he takes to come out of there to decide," he said. "I'd say less than a minute. If you're lucky. Understand?"

She nodded, but her face was a mask of silent confusion.

"I need to get upstairs and speak to your boss. And you need to not get arrested. Am I right?" He didn't wait for her to nod, just ploughed on. "So here's what I propose: you give me full access to this building for the rest of this evening. You will leave immediately and when you return you will never mention me or any of this ever again. In return I will, for the same amount of time, forget about your involvement in any of the crimes I mentioned and you will have a clean slate. What you choose to do with that slate in the morning is, of course, entirely up to you."

The two of them turned to the door as they heard the sound of the paramedic dropping something.

"Ten seconds. What's your answer?" Roach asked.

She nodded.

Roach unlocked and removed the cuffs.

Val reached down to the lanyard that hung around her neck. She slipped a card out from behind her photo ID.

"My card has full access. The lifts, all the doors, all the way up to Mr Croft's office."

She pressed the card into his hand. It was completely blank. Could be anything.

"If you're lying…" Roach let the words hang in the air but he believed her. The way her shoulders hung, the way she rubbed her wrists… it wouldn't surprise him if she was composing a new CV sitting up in bed tonight.

She shook her head.

"Can I go?" she asked. "Please?"

"Help him," said Roach, gesturing to the door behind them. "Once he's gone, you can go too."

"Are we… done?"

"We're done," said Roach and jogged away from her, heading back to his gold reflection in the lifts. "Stay out of trouble." He swiped the card through the receptacle by the lift. For a second, nothing happened and then the tiny red LED on the card reader turned green and he heard the lift's mechanism whirr into life. Moments later the doors slid open silently and he stepped inside.

Val Morris breathed out. She wanted to cry but now was not the time for that. She breathed in and rapped on the door behind her desk.

"Mr nurse man?" she said.

The door opened and the paramedic walked out carrying the small, green box that contained the office medical supplies.

He walked into reception, taking in the sudden change of circumstance that had occurred in his absence.

"Did you kill him?" he grinned.

She stared coldly at him. "Do you have everything

you need, sir?" The years of bureaucratic blustering came back to her faster than the speed of light.

"Yeah, yeah," he replied. "How come you're not arrested then?"

"I just want to go home, if you don't m—"

"Come on. You pay him off?" he winked at her. "Or were you two just playing a bit of the old slap and tickle? Master and servant, eh?"

"Certainly not! It was a… a… misunderstanding." She'd heard somewhere that if you said things with enough conviction eventually you'd believe it yourself.

"I bet it was. Well, thanks for this lot," he said

Val Morris shoved her belongings into her handbag. Her sister had warned her but she hadn't listened. She would go and stay with her in Crowley for a few weeks. Or months.

The paramedic sauntered towards the door, pulling his mobile from his pocket, a grin plastered across his face.

hes in teh lift. u bettr b reddy I'll be in position in 5
Barry

EIGHT

Violet glanced at her phone more out of habit than out of purpose. She noticed the red battery symbol in the corner of the screen. It felt like a betrayal. Except that it wasn't. Not really. The phone was an inanimate object and, as such, lacked the capacity to fall short or aid her. She hadn't turned the charger on at the wall when she plugged it in. She'd thought half a charge was going to be enough. It would be.

Of course it would be, she thought and slipped it back in her pocket, assured that it would last if she could stop habitually checking the bloody thing.

"We need to hurry up," she said, with a smile which said urgency was something that happened to other people.

Katie stood next to the discarded pile of firefighter fatigues in a much more subtle, black outfit. One much more befitting a woman about to engage in nefarious criminal undertakings. That was, however, the only thing subtle about her. At six feet ten inches tall, Katie towered over Violet. As if that wasn't enough Katie trained, and she trained hard, which had given her the muscular build of Bruce Lee. She reached down and ruffled Violet's hair. Violet twisted out of her grasp and glared up at her.

"It's time you got to work," said Violet. She stooped to grab the backpack then brought it up in an arc, throwing it at Katie's head.

Katie caught it with one hand, then reached inside and plucked out a cordless angle grinder, mask and glasses. Securing the safety equipment on her face, she pulled off the plastic guard and revved it a couple of times. She grabbed the filing cabinet Violet had been hiding behind minutes earlier and flung it to one side as if it was nothing more than a cardboard box. Violet glared at her as it brushed past her leg, coming dangerously close to crushing her foot under its very real weight.

Katie's smirk was hidden under her mask as she turned her attention to the wall and attacked it with the angle grinder. Just as the glamour and glitz of the ancient building's facade had stopped outside the public eye, the same level of effort, or lack of it, had been dribbled on the rest of the building. Within moments, she had cut a small door-shaped rectangle in the thin plasterboard. Violet coughed, struggling to find her own mask and eye-protectors from the backpack. When she did finally locate them, she slipped them on and stood, watching Katie.

There was nothing to do but wait. And waiting was boring. Violet rocked backwards and forwards between the heels and the balls of her feet, repeatedly. She looked over to the computer screens. Zoe would be finished covering their tracks by now. Probably. Almost certainly.

She ran through the job timings again in her head. Everything was planned from where she set the first fire to how long it would take them to get through this wall and each subsequent action. She checked her phone. If anything they were ahead of schedule. There was a flicker of mischief amongst the background adrenalin of the job.

The noise stopped abruptly and Violet wondered if that was it. She leaned forward to peer through the gathering dust Katie's efforts were kicking out. The grinder burst back into life and Violet jumped at the sudden intrusion into the silence.

She looked at the computers again and rummaged in the backpack, mischief now firmly on her mind, but almost as quickly as it had started, it was over. Katie discarded the grinder before reaching forward and riving the plasterboard from where it now barely hung, tossing it neatly over Violet's head. It crashed into the computer and she winced for a moment, glancing at Violet and perhaps waiting to be told off.

"Easy, Chewie!" Violet grinned under the mask.

Katie made a low guttural growl and, for a moment, Violet backed down, taking a literal step back, but then mischief got the better of her again and she inched forward as Katie turned her attention to the gap she had created. Behind the plasterboard was a dark wall. Katie surveyed it, calculating whatever it was she calculated way up there in the clouds.

Treading ever-so lightly, Violet padded up to her. Standing on tiptoes, she reached up, trying to twang the elastic on the back of her friend's mask, but it was no good, she couldn't reach. Silently admitting defeat she touched her friend's shoulder.

Katie stopped what she was doing and looked around, tensed. Her eyes flashed with irritation but she shook it off, dropping to one knee and reaching out a hand to touch the wall. Violet followed suit. It was made from foam bricks that were dark grey and ridged. Katie nodded to her and the pair of them grabbed handfuls of the foam and pulled at it. It came away in chunks and soon they had cleared enough to see the red bricks of what would have been the original outside wall of the beautiful Victorian building. The same beautiful Victorian building that government funding had been misappropriated to conceal.

Katie picked up the angle grinder once more and set to work on the bricks as Violet ducked back out of the way. In amongst the screams of blade against stone, Violet checked the CCTV one last time before reaching inside her jacket. Finally she found the item she'd been looking to make her mischief with moments earlier. She pulled out an extendable baton and began by smashing the monitors.

Katie stopped what she was doing and looked over her shoulder at Violet.

"What?" Violet asked. "It's necessary."

Katie continued to stare.

"You know what? Screw you," said Violet in mock-petulance. "I know the screens don't need to be smashed. But it looks good, doesn't it? Like Elias is covering his tracks. And anyway, I just love those breaking noises. Now get on with your job and I'll get on with mine."

The angle grinder howled in protest as it continued its task. It drowned out the sound of Violet smashing the computers and then the hard disks within the computers which held the recordings of the CCTV. A few minutes passed until, finally, Katie was satisfied the hole was large enough. She signalled to Violet, but the air was red, a dust cloud engulfing the office like a localised sand-storm. Squinting into it, she waited, expecting Violet's temporary boredom to manifest itself in another ridiculous attack. She breathed several clammy breaths through her mask, then waved her hand in front of her. After a little wafting the shape of the desk appeared. Then, as the dust settled on the surfaces of the office, Violet popped up from amongst the broken computers, removing her mask and goggles. She blinked an exaggerated wide-eyed blink of innocence. Katie nodded towards the gap in the wall.

Violet snapped back into serious-mode as quickly as she snapped on her torch. She was back in play and wasted no time examining what was in the void Katie had opened up. She peered through the gap, her torch beam flickering into the darkness beyond. The light caught the masonry dust, appearing to propel it through the hole like a swarm of microscopic moths drawn to her light. "We're in," she said.

Katie gave a mock-salute and threw her mask and eye-protectors onto the mangled mess of computers Violet had created. Violet ducked her head, stepping through the space Katie had created out of the Tulip Street Gin Emporium and into the loft space of the building next door.

The smell of the air changed from one building to the next. The masonry, although still there, was replaced with the aroma of damp dust and loft insulation. It reminded Violet of retrieving Christmas decorations from the attic when she was a kid. Katie folded herself through the opening and Violet flashed the torch up at her face before realising she was blinding her and instantly flicking it in another direction.

"Sorry," she said and walked deeper into the loft space.

Katie made to follow her but there was an enormous crash and Violet whirled around, her heart thumping in her chest. For a moment she feared the worst, when the beam of her torch couldn't immediately locate her accomplice, but the rustling, bashing movement soon revealed where her friend was. She moved the torch beam down and it settled on Katie, who was lying on her side amongst the insulation.

"Lazy bitch," said Violet. "We haven't got time for a nap. Stuff to do. Revenge to wreak. All that jazz."

Katie's hand went to cover her mouth as she let out a silent laugh, before standing up and gesturing to the box on the floor she had fallen over. Violet flashed the beam at it. On the side were written the words '7ft Mountain Pine' — it was an actual Christmas tree.

"Seven foot mountain pine." Violet tried to stifle a laugh. "We might have found a new nickname for you."

Katie strode forward, deliberately bumping in to Violet before plucking the torch from her hand. A few strides later and she planted her feet wide apart and flicked the direction of the beam directly between them. Violet moved quickly to catch up, dropping to her knees to inspect the small loft hatch Katie was highlighting. Violet's hands moved to grip the edges of the hatch, but she paused, looking up at her friend. She waited, allowing a silence to engulf them until all that was left was a barely audible ringing in the two women's ears.

Violet allowed her breathing to slow and moved lower and lower, her face closer and closer to the hatch. She nodded to Katie, who shut off the torch, but before either of their eyes could acclimatise to the dark Violet lifted the corner of the loft hatch. Just a crack. Perhaps a centimetre or two.

They waited. Listening. Watching the light. Looking for movement. Expecting to be discovered.

A minute passed without sound, without activity of any kind. Violet lifted the hatch far enough to get a limited view of the room below. No-one was immediately visible. She leaned forward and Katie partially unzipped the backpack on Violet's back, her hand moving so slowly she could feel each tooth in the zipper uncouple. She reached inside and, with the same infinite patience, silently rooted around until she found what she was searching for.

Katie held in her hand what looked for all the world like a length of stiff black wire. She carefully zipped the backpack closed once more before handing the snake camera to Violet, who nodded in acknowledgement.

Violet did as Zoe had shown her, plugging the lead directly into the base of the phone before opening the app and…

1% Battery Remaining

Violet flipped past the warning and activated the app. The screen turned black. For a moment, she thought the phone had let her down. Violet gave the phone a slap and still the screen remained resolutely black.

The pit of her stomach fell but as she moved the end of the wire the light from the room below at last appeared on the screen. Violet realised that she had been holding her breath and tried to breathe normally again. She blinked once, twice and her composure returned. With enormous care, she fed the camera through the hatch and the room below appeared on the phone. The bright light of the screen cast furious shadows on her face as she turned the wire, to rotate the camera, to see the whole of the room.

There was no-one by the closed door. No-one on the plush, velvet seats arranged next to the bookcase.

And then, there was no-one at all. The screen faded, the image of the room collapsing in on itself into a line a single pixel wide and then into darkness once more. Violet took an impatient breath and retracted the camera from the hatch. She held the button on the top of her phone down, knowing as she did it that the damn thing was as dead as they would be if there was someone sitting at the desk in the room.

Violet looked up to Katie, whose head was cocked judgementally to one side.

"Well I don't suppose you brought yours, did you?" she whispered.

Katie gave a small shake of the head.

"Plan B," said Violet. "We do this the old-fashioned way."

Katie flipped her the bird.

Violet ignored her and leaned forward, her head resting on the rough wood of the hatch's frame.

She could see the door to the room was still closed. Her field of vision, limited though it was, remained mercifully free of any living, breathing person. She looked up at Katie, her face barely visible in the darkness, and nodded. She saw the up-down movement of the nod in return.

Changing her grip on the loft hatch, Violet held it open with her right hand, her left held splayed in the air above her head.

Five

Her eyes adjusted and she could see Katie's expression of concentration.

Four

Violet was counting down on her fingers, Katie nodding in time with each digit she dropped.

Three

Eyes fixed on the tiny sliver of the room below, Violet knew if they were discovered too early this would all have been a spectacular waste of time. And a waste of time that could cost her her life.

Two

No turning back now.

One

Violet whipped the loft hatch off completely and, in the same instant, Katie dropped down through it and into the relative unknown of the room below.

NINE

THERE HAD BEEN no sound from the room beneath Violet for at least a minute. She began to gradually move back towards the open loft hatch.

"Katie?" Violet breathed.

No noise came from the room below.

"Katie?" Violet moved closer still, unable to see her friend through the hatch.

"Katie?" she said, louder this time.

There was no reply. This was not a huge surprise, given that Katie was mute, but there was something else about the silence. Something Violet didn't like. She should have been able to hear her friend moving. Nonetheless, she couldn't wait any longer. If her friend was in danger then she had to face the threat head on.

Head on and upside down in this case.

Violet lowered herself into the room so that her hair entered first, hanging below her inverted face. She whipped her head around, taking in the whole room from the door and bookcase she had already seen to the wall opposite, where a well-stocked drinks cabinet sat under a portrait of a man who appeared to be Napoleon. Looking past the uniform and focussing on the face Violet smirked, realising that Elias Croft had had himself painted in place of the little man. She turned her attention to Croft's desk. The wide, mahogany monstrosity was inlaid with red leather and sat in front of a wall made entirely of glass. A huge, dark red leather chair sat behind the desk and, leaning back in it with her legs crossed, feet perched on the inlaid red leather of the desk, nudging a metal pen jutting from a holder attached to it, was Katie. And she was reading a book.

"What the hell are you doing?" Violet spat the words.

Katie ignored her, preferring to make an exaggerated motion of licking her thumb and turning the page.

Violet dumped her backpack on the desk, lowered herself down and surveyed the room from a right-side-up perspective. There was a fireplace along one wall and above it was a huge oil painting of the film star Bruno Zenker in his signature role as Gino Lombardi from the movie 'I Am The Mob'. Lombardi was a particularly vicious Italian-American gangster, primarily because he was a bit of a short-arse.

"He's very fond of Zenker, isn't he?" asked Violet.

Katie didn't respond.

"He was from Kilchester, you know? Back then he

was called Wilbur Wimberley," said Violet. "I read one of his biographies. You wouldn't keep a name like that, would you? Wilbur Wimberley."

Katie tapped the page of the book she was reading, but Violet carried on unperturbed as she walked around the office, getting a feel for the room. "I mean there was no shaking Kilchester's stink from her favourite son but Zenker seemed to embrace the infatuations the idiots from this city had with him and, sort of, played with it."

Violet looked along the spines of the books on one of the shelves, then pulled one out.

"This is the biography, if you'd like to read it?" she asked.

Katie gave a slight shake of her head and made a show of turning another page in her own book.

"Like so many actors, he always mentioned his home town when he was interviewed," said Violet, flicking through the book. "But he made sure he never came back here unless there was absolutely, unequivocally no alternative."

Violet ran her fingers lightly along the mantelpiece. The wood looked like it could be ebony and black tiles ran along the wall under the painting. She paused to look at a single, rectangular, plastic tile that was embedded into the wood. The perfectly presented fire was just a pile of neatly chopped logs in a hearth that looked like it had never been lit. Next to it was a stand with cast iron tools for stoking and cleaning the fire, none of which showed signs of scorching or dirt.

"He won an Oscar for that," said Violet, then

snapped the book shut and put it back on the shelf. She'd hoped to startle Katie. Instead, Katie closed her own book and nodded towards the painting of Zenker.

"Yes," said Violet, with mounting irritation. "That's him."

Katie made a turning gesture with her fingers.

"Nah," replied Violet, lifting the painting slightly to look behind. "Nothing there — it'll be behind the other one."

Katie raised her eyebrows, but no emotion was visible in her expression.

"After the Oscar there was the inevitable drink and drug decline," said Violet as she walked her fingers around the frame of the fake Napoleon, carefully checking for any obvious alarm triggers, and then lifted the painting down from the wall.

"Ta da!" Violet did a little curtsey as she pointed to the safe.

Katie gave a light round of applause and leaned further back in her chair.

Violet examined the safe more closely as Katie went back to her book.

"He went," she continued, as she examined every millimetre of the safe, "from award-winning must-have to washed-up has-been in less than a decade."

The safe was perhaps a metre along each side and inset into the wall so that the electronic keypad didn't stand proud. Beneath the numbers of the keypad was a large handle which Violet tugged. It didn't budge.

"And then along came Bunny," said Violet.

She thought for a moment, then unzipped her hoodie, searching hidden compartments until she pulled out an eight inch strip of thin metal. It looked like a metal ruler, but as Violet worked it, it became apparent that it had some, but not much, flexibility. She bent one end slightly, inspecting it and working it some more until she was satisfied with the angle. Then she forced it through the tiny gap between the edge of the safe and its door.

"You know," said Violet, her words stilted by her efforts with the safe, "you're supposed… to be the muscle… you could… y'know… act like it… be on guard or… something."

Katie turned another page.

"Fine," said Violet as she pushed the piece of metal further and further into the safe. "Bunny was twenty-five years his junior. Yes, she was a blonde. Yes, she exuded stupidity from every pore, but scratch the surface and the opposite was true." Violet kept working the ruler into the safe, millimetre by millimetre. "Bunny single-handedly put him back on the map. Networked. Got him noticed by the coolest kids on the block and he ended up in some fantastic films. Did you see 'Angry Monday'?"

Katie looked up from her book long enough to shake her head.

"Of course you didn't," muttered Violet. "Probably in the gym. Well, it was good."

Katie shrugged.

"Zenker was prone to self-destruction though. Went

into what I like to call the 'racist grandad' period of his career." Violet stopped working the metal ruler in, satisfied with the progress she'd made shoving it into the safe, and instead moved it up and down, feeling for something. "He broke up with Bunny and moved in with his plastic surgeon."

As her hands worked, Violet's eyes stared almost blankly at the ceiling, picturing the inside of the safe in her head as she spoke.

"That plastic surgeon was a woman of singular determination. She seemed hell-bent on nipping and tucking him until his facial skin was so tight he could barely blink."

Violet's movements were getting smaller, as if she was closing in on whatever it was she was trying to reach.

"He cut Bunny out of his will… mostly," she said. "But in an almost certainly drug-related twist of fate, Zenker left her three things: his poodle, which was also called Bunny, his Oscar statuette and, for reasons that never became clear, his ashes."

Katie placed the book on the desk once more, apparently finally interested by what Violet was saying.

"She had the dog put down," said Violet.

Katie made a face like she'd just tasted bitter lemon.

"She sold the Oscar and his ashes to the highest bidder. And those bids were pretty high because Zenker was the darling of the criminal fraternity."

Katie looked bemused.

"Must be a male thing," said Violet. "Not exactly the

darling of the criminal sorority. Is that a thing? That should be a thing."

Katie nodded.

"And then we stole it. The urn with the ashes, I mean," she said, a smile forming on her face. "Anyway, watch…"

Katie steepled her fingers, all dutiful obedience. Violet put pressure on the metal strip before typing a sequence of numbers into the safe's keypad.

1 - 2 - 3 - 4 - 5 - 6

There was a beep and a green light flashed. Violet turned the handle, and the door swung open.

Katie looked mightily unimpressed.

"No!" protested Violet, a little too loudly. "That wasn't the code."

Katie's brow furrowed and she stood up.

"You see," said Violet, throwing open the door as wide as it would go. "There's a button here." She pointed to the rim of the door.

Katie wasn't watching. She stalked from behind the desk, past Violet, to the office door.

"And when you hold the button down," said Violet, but the enthusiasm drained from her voice with every word until she reached a deliberate robotic monotone, "you can reset the passcode. But I did it with the door closed."

Katie was staring at the closed door, listening to something outside.

"Which is really impressive," Violet muttered to no-one in particular. "Because most safes don't have that."

Katie snapped her fingers and pointed urgently to the door.

Violet nodded, snapping back into job-mode. She reached into the safe and grabbed an armful of the contents, dumping them on the desk before repeating the process two more times. Meanwhile, Katie left her post guarding the door and grabbed Violet's backpack. Reaching into it, she took out a bundle of twenty pound notes wrapped with a money band. She flicked through the thousand-pound wad and threw it into the safe.

Shoving her hand into the backpack, she pulled out another fistful of the thousand-pound bundles. She paused, her eyes darting to Violet's back.

"I'm perfectly aware that you don't think this is a very good idea," said Violet.

Katie pursed her lips in irritation.

"Have I ever let you down?" asked Violet, a little more softly but somehow managing to inject a little menace into the question.

Katie resumed shoving fistfuls of thousand-pound bundles into the safe.

There was a sound at the door. Both women snapped their heads around to look. Someone was out there.

"You ready?" asked Violet.

Katie shrugged.

"Oh, piss off," said Violet, loudly this time so the people on the other side of the door could hear.

Katie grinned and the door swung open.

The look on Elias Croft's face when he walked through bore scant resemblance to his Napoleonic portrait. Poise and battlefield composure was replaced with a hang-jawed double-take.

Violet and Katie stood still. Elias stood still. They stared. He gawped. And then, like air rushing into a vacuum, his wits returned to him and all hell broke loose.

80

TEN

THE LIFT WASN'T AS big as Roach had thought it would be. The upper-halves were mirrored on every side, creating an infinite crowd of doppelgangers, all standing uncomfortably close and looking more than a little guilty for the actions which had brought them into possession of a staff key card. As the doors slid quietly closed, Roach pressed the button for the top floor. A living cliché like Croft would have the penthouse office, there was no doubt in the detective's mind.

Roach didn't yet have a plan for when the doors opened. Still, there was plenty of time to come up with one. A minute. Maybe two.

Roach's mobile vibrated in his pocket, snapping him out of his reverie. He slid it out and suppressed a groan as the name of his partner flashed up on the screen. He swiped and answered.

"Addison?" Roach said.

"Where are you?" asked Scarfe.

"Same place I was before," tried Roach.

"And where's that?" Scarfe persisted.

"On the scene. Same place I was before, like I said. What did you want? I'm sort of in the middle of something."

"So you're not in Croft's building?"

Roach's shoulder dropped and he closed his eyes in frustration. How did they *always* know?

"There was a report. I'm investigating," he said, his voice belying the irritation churning through his bloodstream.

"Investigating something is a two-man job," said Scarfe. It was a statement. It was *always* a statement.

"I'm en route to his office," said Roach, stabbing at the button for the top floor once more in the vain hope it would speed the lift. "I'll meet you there." He hung up, checked his phone and then spoke to the black mirror in his hand, "Like you would know the first thing about investigating, you corrupt fuck."

Roach shelved his irritation as the lift jerked to a halt and the doors slid open. If money had been spent downstairs, it had been melted down and splattered across the walls up here. The corridor was wide and long, with only a handful of doors leading off it. The floor felt like it could be sprung, the dark wood parquet polished to a reflective sheen. The doors on the left and right each had brass plaques to the side but the door at the end of the corridor was unlabelled. And open.

Roach could see Elias and two black-suited men entering that far room. Pacing down the corridor, the bounce in his step increased with each stride. He pushed aside the urge to throw in a couple of ill-advised dance steps. Keep your eye on the target.

Which was exactly what he did, his eye firmly planted on his quarry as the two bodyguards and Croft closed the heavy door behind them.

But Roach didn't have to rush. He slowed his steps and tapped his pocket reassuringly. In there was a warrant card. And if that didn't work there was the access card. He paused a few feet from the door, composing himself and ordering his thoughts. The door was significantly larger, in both width and height, than any of the others. Almost as if Croft had something to prove with every part of the building that he could not with his own anatomy.

Deciding that the warrant card would go ignored from the outset, Roach plucked the access card from his pocket and ran it through the black plastic receptacle near the door handle. There was no light. No red, no green, nothing.

He rubbed the magnetic strip with his thumb and ran it through a second time. Again there wasn't even a flicker of recognition.

He turned the card upside down and swiped it again. A green light flashed twice and then a solid red light. The door didn't unlock.

The detective gave the card one last swipe, but again the solid red light mocked him and the door remained resolutely locked.

Oh well, he thought, time to do this the old-fashioned way. He raised his clenched fist and rapped on the door.

And then something odd happened. All hell broke loose inside the room. For a moment, Roach imagined that he had caught them in the middle of something nefarious, and that they were so scared of him that his knock alone had sent them into a panic. He soon realised, however, that the panic and the shouting was nothing to do with him. Something else was happening in the room. He needed to find out what it was, so he placed his ear against the flat of the door and listened.

ELEVEN

ELIAS SCREAMED orders and two men who looked like they were built from anger and ball-bearings barged into the room, flanking him and wielding pistols like they actually knew what to do with them. Once his mook's guns were trained on Violet and Katie, Elias' cool returned like an elastic band twanging back into shape.

Violet he recognised, of course. The other one he hadn't seen before. Their appearance was unexpected, but he had a lid on it now. He walked behind his desk, slamming his shoulder into Violet as he walked past. He was pleased to see she didn't dare react. Elias bent over and opened the bottom desk drawer, from which he retrieved a bag of zip-ties.

"Miss Winters," he said, tossing the zip-ties to his guards.

"Mister Croft," Violet replied. One of the meatsacks pulled her hands together behind her back and wrapped the plastic tie around them, pulling it tight so it cut into her skin. Violet winced in pain.

"And your friend? I don't believe I've had the pleasure."

"And you're not likely to," said Violet. "She's the silent type."

Katie's guard yanked her arms behind her back then pulled the zip-tie around her wrists. She didn't react.

"On your knees, both of you," said Elias as he examined the chaos the pair had created. "How did you get in here?"

"Oh, you know me," said Violet. "I can walk through walls."

Elias' eyes flashed around the room, looking for any indications of incursion.

They never look up, she thought.

"I thought our business was concluded," said Elias. He walked over to the painting of Zenker and adjusted the angle slightly, before running his hand lightly across the mantelpiece.

"There was a problem," said Violet.

"Oh?" Elias sat himself down in the chair behind his desk.

"You paid me with monopoly money, you fat fuck."

Elias slapped his hands on the desk and let out a short, loud laugh. "Monopoly. Very good." He bared his teeth in a mock-smile. "Money is money. Even counterfeit. You could have spent it."

"Not the point. You hired me because of my reputation, and I don't want a reputation for accepting funny money."

"So, what… you decided to give it back to me? You dumb bitch."

86

Katie inhaled sharply and glanced at Violet, who countered with a micro-shake of her head.

"Oh, and I bet you thought there'd be some real cash in the safe, so you could make a little trade, teach me a lesson?" he continued.

"Something like that," said Violet.

"And you think you have a reputation?" He laughed and turned to Katie. "Are you part of this reputation?"

Katie shrugged her left shoulder.

"Answer me," he said and gestured to Katie's guard, who slapped her across the cheek. It flared red but she didn't react. "Answer me!" he screamed.

"I told you, you porridge-brained little shit," said Violet. "She's the silent type. She doesn't speak. Ever."

Elias stared at her for a long moment, as if the concept she was introducing him to was a bullet made of jelly fired right at his stupid face. He shook his head.

"Never mind that," he said, this time gesturing to Violet's guard who, in turn, slapped her.

"Slapping? Really?" asked Violet, spitting a gob of blood onto Elias' pristine carpet. She watched the weave of the wool absorb it, instantaneously turning liquid into stain, then she cleared her throat and affected a shrill, mocking tone. "Oh I'm Elias Croft the big, bad gangster and the only thing I can think of to deal with a woman who's cleverer than me is to slap her…"

Elias stared at her again, the processors in his brain overheating with the effort of trying to calculate what the hell her game was. In the end, he gave up and went for the direct approach.

"What do you think will happen here?" he asked.

"You break into my office and get yourselves caught. Do you think I'm going to let you both go?"

Violet grinned. "Is that what you think is happening?"

Elias stood up behind his desk. "I don't care what's happening. *I'm* what's happening."

Violet laughed and looked across at Katie, who smirked back at her.

"*He's* what's happening," Violet mimicked. "That doesn't even make sense."

Elias was turning a novel shade of mauve.

"If I say I'm what's happening, then I *am* what's happening. Shut up. Hit them both again."

The sound of hand against cheek echoed around the room once more, followed once more by Violet's laughter. The guard wasn't happy about the laughter and balled his hand up into a fist, punching her once, twice in the face. Blood ran from her nose and mouth. With the bruises blooming on her eye and cheeks, she looked like something from a horror film.

Violet tilted her head left, then right, as if stretching the muscles in her neck. This time, when she smiled there was a crimson outline to each of her white teeth.

"What's happening is that we are putting this money here to frame you. Once that's taken care of, we'll walk out of here with Zenker's ashes and then—"

Elias was whooping with laughter now. "You! You'll *frame* me?" Tears streamed down his face. "You?" He banged his fists on the desk and walked unsteadily over to Zenker's painting.

A seriousness settled on him like lies on a

clairvoyant. "Looks like I've pissed on your party then, doesn't it?" he growled, waving a hand at the two women trussed and on their knees.

"So it would seem," said Violet and then, mustering her best *I'm definitely not being sarcastic* voice, she added, "You've certainly outsmarted us."

Elias, too eager to believe what she was saying, didn't look back at her. "Tell me, how would I even get arrested? The police in this town are as bent as…" he trailed off, metaphors failing him.

"Not all of them," said Violet.

"Perhaps not, but that's hardly the point now, is it?"

And right then, Violet knew she had him. Flustered, confused, but more importantly cocksure. All she had to do was give him one last prod and he would do the rest of the work for her.

"I suppose not. And anyway, you had me completely foxed," said Violet, her eyes scanning the room. "I found your safe, but I would never have found Zenker's ashes."

"Of course you wouldn't." Elias puffed out his chest and threw back his shoulders. "And even if you'd found where I kept them, you wouldn't have been able to get at them."

"Oh yeah?"

"Oh yeah," he sneered.

"Bet I could."

"Nope."

"How come?"

"You would have needed this."

He held up his thumb.

"What do you mean?" Violet asked, frowning. "I'd need evidence that you have a tiny penis?"

Elias moved to hit her himself this time, but the bloodied mess he'd already made of her face seemed to give him pause. And then he smirked. Pleased with himself for teaching this troublesome woman a lesson. His eyes flicked from his prisoners to their guards, still standing with their pistols drawn.

Violet caught the smirk and sucked air through her teeth.

"Well, I can't stick around all day I'm afraid," said Violet. "Boring conversation anyway…" And then she added with sudden animation. "Katie, you're up."

"Wha—" Elias began, his head cocked to one side in confusion.

Katie got to her feet and the shouting started once more. First Elias, shouting to the guards to subdue her. Then the guards themselves. Ordering her to get down, the bullying tone in the voices stretching, raising in pitch as she rose in height, the guns waving at her as if they were made of rubber. Katie pulled her hands apart sharply and the zip-ties fell to the floor.

She rubbed first at her left wrist, then her right, massaging the red marks the ties had created, then she took a long, deep breath. Only two of the men were an immediate threat. Her own guard was a couple of metres in front of her, Violet's guard more to the middle of the room, also out of immediate striking distance. The unarmed Elias lay beyond them.

Katie bent down in the pose a runner would adopt on the blocks. The volume of the shouting reduced at what the men assumed was a pose of supplication. She waited a moment for them to relax, before shooting out her right hand and grabbing the poker from its holder by the fireside. With unerring accuracy she hurled it towards Violet's guard. It spun through the air, slamming into the back of his hand and catching his forearm for good measure. The result was exactly as she expected. Violet's guard dropped his gun and clutched at his arm, the metacarpal bone definitely bruised, probably fractured.

Katie *hadn't* expected the guard to burst into tears, but there was sometimes an unexpected bonus in these situations.

She rose to her full height once more, as her own guard advanced on her, gun outstretched, safety off, ready to shoot. Looking at the trajectory of where he was pointing if he pulled the trigger, it would hit her in the gut. Not ideal. She moved forward too, opening up her arms a little, flexing her considerable muscle to show this little wannabe exactly what he was dealing with. He wasn't scared, kept coming, arm straight, ready to fire.

Well, he wasn't scared yet.

Katie raised her hands in mock-surrender. The gun was only a metre away now. If he pulled the trigger they'd be unlikely to get an ambulance to her quickly enough to stop her bleeding out.

No need to worry, though.

She lunged forward, almost clapping her hands together over the gun. Almost. But not quite. Her left hand grabbed the barrel, her right hand the butt and she twisted it, still in the guard's grip, through one hundred and eighty degrees. At the same time she yanked the gun towards her so it was down by her side, the muzzle pointing safely at the wall behind her.

The guard's face changed, his jaw hanging open in fear and surprise, then a millisecond later contorting in pain as Katie carried through. The guard continued gripping the gun and Katie continued to turn it, which had the effect of doubling him over onto his knees, his arm locked straight in her grip as she lifted the gun higher. The air filled with screams once more, but this time not the screaming of demands. These were the screams of panic. Katie twisted the gun further and the butt came out of the guard's palm, but his finger was still in the metal of the trigger guard. She stared him in the eye as she lifted his arm up high in the air then puckered her lips and blew him a little kiss as she gave the gun one final twist.

It came loose with a crack like dry twigs. Katie held the gun upside down, the barrel lying flat in her hand. She looked down at the whimpering guard, writhing on the floor at her feet. After a moment, he seemed to come to his senses and used his feet to push himself backwards, away from this monster. He clutched his hand to his chest and Katie assessed the damage. His index finger hung as flaccid and loose as spaghetti. Proximal phalanges shattered beyond repair. Middle and distal phalanges almost certainly broken too. She eyed him carefully. Despite the screaming and howling, he wasn't done. There was a hatred, a fury, scorching his eyes.

Usually they just passed out at this point. This hateful, furious behaviour was most disagreeable.

His howling was showing potential that it might reach a height only dogs could hear, and yet still he continued. His back reaching the solid wood of the desk, he pushed himself upright. He slapped his undamaged left hand on the wood, whatever he was trying to do clearly a work in progress, but progressing nonetheless.

No. She wasn't going to have that.

The guard winced as Katie took a step towards him. She plucked the metal fountain pen from its holder. The guard's hand remained splayed, flat on the desk as he tried to leverage himself to his feet. He looked up at her cold, blank, expression and for a split second was silent, his face contorting into a mask of pleading. But it was a plea that was not to be granted, as Katie slammed the pen into the back of his hand, lodging it firmly in the wood of the desk beneath. At last the screaming stopped, as the guard's body could no longer take the pain and he passed out.

Katie gave a little nod as if mentally ticking a task off an internal to-do list, before her gaze tracked to Violet who was, by now, lying on her side on the floor, completely unable to get out of the zip-ties. Katie raised a judgemental eyebrow.

"Shut up and get on with it," was all Violet said as she repeatedly yanked at her bonds.

Katie smirked and shrugged, turning back to the first guard. His head went left and right and left and right until he saw what he was looking for; the gun he'd dropped. Katie shook her head and pretended to jump forward. The guard flinched and backed away before awkwardly reaching inside his coat with his left hand and pulling out a knife. Katie shook her head once more and waggled the, albeit upside down, gun in her left hand at him.

The guard gave this a moment's thought before Katie pulled back like a shot put thrower and launched the weapon at him. The pistol arced through the air and struck him square between the eyes. There was a nasty noise, like a hammer hitting a brick, and the guard fell to the floor, the consciousness drained out of him.

"Your left hand? Really?" sneered Violet.

Katie turned to her, her face as innocent and comical as a sniggering child. She lifted her right hand and swiped twice through the air, as if she was holding a rapier.

"Over too quickly is a bloody dumb excuse. You spend too much time watching movies."

Katie rolled her eyes and stalked over to her latest victim, giving him a nudge with her foot before collecting the knife and both the guns from the ground. Turning around, she stood over Violet, who had managed to get her hands in front of her but was still firmly trussed. Katie raised her eyebrows at her friend.

"I know you told me how to do this," said Violet, "but, no, I can't get out."

Katie dropped the knife and the tip embedded itself in the floor between Violet's feet. Violet glared at her. Katie grinned and gave her a wink before spinning around to deal with Elias.

"Yes!" said Violet to Katie's back. "Didn't need the knife. I got there in the end. On my own. Without it."

Violet stood up, shook off her ridiculous sense of accomplishment, and walked over to stand side by side with Katie.

"Would you like my colleague to stamp on your fucking throat?" Violet asked Elias, sweetly.

Katie stared at him, waiting for the response. It came in an instant — a massive adrenaline dump that set his legs twitching.

"No," he whimpered, shaking his head a little too long.

Violet gestured to the bodies of the two guards and Katie gave an exaggerated sigh as she grabbed two zip-ties from the bag on the desk, then dragged her feet over to the farthest of the prone guards with all the grace of a sullen teenager.

"Whu…" Elias' mouth was moving, but not many actual sounds were coming out. "What…"

Violet rearranged her face into a fake smile. "Aw, sweetie," she said, spilling saccharine-sweet sarcasm. "Did you think the little girlies were here to stomp our ickle feetie-weeties?"

She shoved out her bottom lip and pretended to wring the tears out of her eyes. Behind her, Katie had placed the first guard neatly against the wall.

"Listen, I haven't been entirely honest with you," said Violet, catching Elias' gaze and bringing it back to her and away from Katie. "I wanted you to catch us in the act."

"It—" Elias didn't get any further than a single syllable.

"The safe was easy for a woman of my not inconsiderable talents." Violet pretended to polish her nails on her lapel and inspect them. "And we brought back all of the crap you paid us with." She riffled a stack of notes in the safe, picking out a few bundles and throwing them to Katie, who shoved them in the guard's jacket pockets.

Violet took another handful of notes and wandered over to the second guard, his body still hanging awkwardly from the hand skewered to the desk. "For your trouble," she said, scattering the bundles of fake cash around his feet.

"You see, when the police arrive they're going to find you have an awful lot of this monopoly money on your person, so you're going to be in a bit of bother."

"That's your plan?" he began quietly. "Don't make me laugh." He still sounded a country mile away from being able to laugh, like a little boy threatening the headmistress, but his self-assurance was returning. "I own more cops than you own pairs of shoes, love."

"Oh no," said Violet, shocking him into silence once more. "My well laid plan is suddenly and irrevocably ruined by your insightful mansplaining."

He stared at her, his eyebrows shifting about on his brow like two trucks performing synchronised parking manoeuvres.

"You think I'd have come this far and not taken that into account?" Violet continued.

His eyes burning with hatred, he shook his head just enough to acknowledge Violet's question.

Katie towered behind Violet, cocking her head to one side to take in the broken, drooped form of the remaining guard. Elias eyed her nervously.

Violet clicked her fingers in front of his face, bringing him back into the moment, forcing him to focus. To listen. "Concentrate, shit for brains. I'm talking. She's not talking, *I am*."

Katie turned to look at Elias and gave him a resigned smile.

"Let me get this straight," he said. "You know that I can buy my way out of this, but you did it anyway?"

Violet nodded then pulled her shoulders in tight, grinned and put her hand over her mouth. "Tee hee!" she said.

Behind Violet, Katie had braced her foot against the desk and was tugging at the pen in the back of the guard's hand. With every tug, Elias gagged.

"Not feeling too well?"

Elias' cheeks puffed out for a moment as a caustic discharge burned its way up his throat, but he swallowed it down.

Katie gave one final tug and the pen came out, flying loose and spiralling over her shoulder through the air, spattering a cartwheel of blood as it went.

"Fuck's sake, Katie!" Violet snapped in mock-anger, but as she looked back to Elias, she saw he had a trail of blood streaked diagonally from his chin over the grid of hair plugs on top of his head. His legs continued to shake and a dark patch had formed around the crotch of his trousers. Violet's nose wrinkled as the smell of urine drifted upwards. "Eew. Have you pissed in your pants? I thought we were dealing with proper gangsters." She turned to Katie, who had hoisted the damaged guard into her arms before stacking him on top of his colleague, like they were a pair of sofa cushions. "You would have thought he'd be used to this kind of thing?"

The corners of Katie's mouth turned down and a thoughtful look drifted across her face, before she gave a light shrug.

Violet turned back to Elias. His entire head was pale, his whole body shaking.

"Don't usually go out without your guards, eh?" asked Violet.

Elias shook his head.

"Wise move. You really never know what could happen to you. Especially when you go around ripping off honest, hard-working criminals."

"What are you going to do?" Elias asked, the fight drained out of him and soaked into the carpet. "To me," he added, looking at Katie.

"Glad you asked." Violet clapped her hands enthusiastically. "I've prepared a little song for this bit. Hit it, Katie!" She pointed to her companion and waved a single jazz hand with her other.

"Not…" there was a long pause between Elias' first word and his second. "Really?"

"Of course not really," said Violet, dropping her hands back to her sides. "Where was I? Oh yes, I explained the whole funny money payback, didn't I?"

He nodded.

"Good. Well the second thing was... I want Zenker's ashes back. I'm not in the habit of stealing things for free and I've lined up a new buyer. I should thank you for that, though."

Elias frowned in confusion.

"That was the whole point of our little charade. I mean, we could have found where you had hidden the urn eventually and bypassed the thumbprint scanner but it seemed like overkill when we could just... let Katie flex her muscles."

"Is she—"

Katie cracked her knuckles and Elias stopped talking.

"Where was I?" Violet pretended to ask Katie. "Ah yes, so funny money placed, arrest arranged, urn retrieved..." She pretended to look around the room. "Wait a minute. Silly me. I haven't retrieved the urn. Not yet."

Elias stared at her in fear and incomprehension.

"Press the button and give me the urn or Katie will pull off your arms and beat you to death with the wet ends."

Katie stopped what she was doing to give Elias a sad little nod.

"I believe she will," he whispered, almost to himself, before squelching a couple of steps to the mantelpiece. Reluctantly, Elias pressed his thumb against the single plastic tile embedded into the wood under the painting. The pristine pile of neatly chopped logs masquerading as a fire in the hearth slid out of sight, revealing a hidden compartment.

Elias reached inside, but hesitated when he heard Katie sucking air through her teeth.

"She's right," said Violet. "How do we know there's not a gun or something in there. You go back to your patch of piss, where we can see you, and I'll—" Violet was interrupted by Katie putting her hand on her arm.

She pointed at her own chest then towards the hearth. Violet nodded in return, acknowledging the superior skill of her friend in dealing with weapons and traps, should there be any.

Inside the hearth was a box covered with black silk, the material held in place with studs that were most likely actual gold rather than simply gold in colour. Katie held one of her huge hands under its base, the other holding the side so it didn't tip over, and placed the box on the desk before unfastening the matching gold clasp. Contained within was an item they both recognised; the urn containing the ashes of Zenker. Katie lifted the lid and poked her finger inside, stirring the gritty contents absent-mindedly. Violet gave a little cough and her friend withdrew her disrespectful digit, screwing the urn's lid on tightly. Katie pulled a 'sorry' face, before putting the urn in their backpack and handing a couple more bundles of notes to Violet.

"Ah yes," said Violet. She moved towards Elias but stopped as she reached the damp patch he was standing in. "If you were a puppy I'd probably get her to rub your nose in that." She walked around to his side, finding a dry patch and leaning over to place the bundles in his pocket. "The thing is... I'm very much aware that here, right now, we hold the cards. I'm also perfectly aware that once we leave you'll get… ideas."

Elias' face had flushed with anger once more.

"And I'm willing to bet that those ideas would centre around doing awful things to me and her. And that's why I decided to kill your only source of income. Kill it with fire."

"The club?" he whispered. "The fire was… you?"

Violet nodded.

"I should—" Elias began, the fight starting to light inside him once more.

"You should be thankful we didn't burn down your house with you inside of it."

He pouted and then, slowly, a smile crept onto his face.

Violet watched it. Waiting for the thoughts to form in his head before she plucked them out and crushed them.

"You're thinking about the insurance, aren't you?" Violet asked.

The smile paused, frozen on his face. "How did you—"

"It's like you don't know me at all," she said and then, turning to Katie she continued. "I honestly feel a little insulted as to how underestimated I'm feeling right now."

Katie shrugged innocently.

"Actually, we increased your insurance," said Violet.

"You did what?" Elias wasn't following and Violet was loving it.

"Yeah we called the insurers up, pretended to be you

and increased your coverage. But only on fire damage. You were pretty worried about your club burning down. Your office too as I recall."

He squinted at her in confusion.

"Buuuut…" said Violet before he could think any more thoughts. "We also hacked your CCTV. So you left this office five minutes before the fire started. Were seen on camera in the places where the fire started at the time it started and then you came back in here to pretend you didn't know anything about it."

"But how…" he trailed off.

"How? Like I said before. By being cleverer than you. It's really not hard. We just spliced footage of you from yesterday. My team is very, very good."

Katie pretended to grab an imaginary pair of lapels and gave a smile of appreciation.

"If it spreads into this building—"

"And it will."

"—I'll lose everything"

"Yep."

"I'll—"

"You'll what? When you wake up, you won't have the money to bribe your way out of anything. And with no club, there'll be no coming back."

"Wake up?"

"Yeah, sorry about that," said Violet. "The next part of the plan sort of requires you to be unconscious."

"Un—"

Katie's fist slammed into Elias' cheekbone. He was unconscious before his eyelids closed, his body limp and lifeless. He might have dropped to the ground like a bowel-full of elephant shit, but Katie had really put her back into the blow. As a result, the impact of the punch launched Elias at the door, the other side of his head smashing into it as he collapsed in a heap on the carpet.

Katie looked over to Violet, who gave her a grin and a little round of applause. "I think our work here is done," she said, pulling on her backpack. "Now, give me a bunk up, will you? I can't reach the hatch."

Katie ignored her for a moment and grabbed the book she had been reading from the desk. She turned to Violet, her eyebrows raised in question.

"You're asking me if you can take it?" asked Violet.

Katie nodded.

"Katie, we're criminals. We don't ask to take stuff. That's kind of in the job description."

Katie slipped the book into Violet's backpack and zipped it closed, then lifted Violet into the air.

TWELVE

DETECTIVE ROACH STOOD STILL, ear pressed to the door, listening. The initial shouting had subsided and had given way to a conversation, although the office door was too thick for Roach to make out what they were saying.

The lift doors at the other end of the corridor slid open and his partner, Scarfe, strode from the lift and down the corridor in his direction.

"Have any trouble getting in?" asked Roach.

Scarfe shook his head.

"No one on the front desk?"

Scarfe shook his head. "Why?" he asked, suspiciously.

"I pointed out the error of her ways. Explained to her the sort of person she's working for," said Roach.

"I've... dealt with her before," Scarfe replied. "She brought your antics to my attention when she saw me outside."

Roach curled his hand into a fist and dug his nails

into his palm. He knew what that meant. It meant that Scarfe had been involved in something dodgy in these premises. It meant that the secretary recognised him as someone the criminals could trust and it meant that Roach was the threat. None of which was a huge surprise, but he couldn't help the red mist descending at the thought.

He took a breath. This time, tonight, there was a chance he could do something in spite of all that.

"So what's going on?" asked Scarfe.

Roach took his ear away from the door. "There was someone in there. Maybe more than one person. Elias and two guards interrupted them and now the door's locked."

Scarfe reached into his pocket, retrieving his own swipe card and pulled it gently through the card reader. Roach stared at the lights, waiting for Scarfe's access to outstrip his own. The green light flashed once, twice but the red light followed and the door once more remained resolutely closed.

"It's—" Roach stopped abruptly at the unmistakable sound of Elias and his two guards shouting. There was a rising panic in the room on the other side of the door.

The slightly smug, condescending look that Scarfe had been wearing fell away and he re-swiped his card. Once, twice, three times he pulled it through the scanner, but each time the red light denied him entry.

There was an explosion of activity in the room and then the unmistakable sound of a grown man sobbing.

"I'm calling in the troops," said Scarfe, looking more alarmed than Roach had seen him before.

His partner maintained a certain poise, a silent menace. He was part of the boys' club and Roach was not. He could get what he wanted, could negotiate with criminals and release them without charge. He was part of a system that worked for money, not justice, and yet here he was, unnerved.

Roach wondered whether it was because Elias Croft had something on Scarfe, or whether this was something that would put a future pay day in jeopardy. Whatever it was, the alarm remained even when the uniformed officers piled out of the lift, the man leading them carrying a bright red battering ram. Down the side, scrawled in white paint, were the words 'knock knock'.

"Sir, we need to be quick," said the lead officer. "The fire's spread to the ground floor of this building. The whole place is gonna burn, according to the water fairies."

"Well we need to get in here," said Scarfe, standing to one side. "There are civilians."

The officer with the battering ram raised an eyebrow to Roach at the mention of the word 'civilians'. He knew as well as anyone what the score was. Elias was a fully paid-up member of the untouchable gang, so his door was not to be kicked in without a bloody good reason.

The gathered detectives and officers stood back to give him room and the officer swung the ram into the door. One blow sent the lock mechanism splintering through the wooden door frame. The door swung open and the two detectives stepped through.

Inside, a strange tableau presented itself. Elias'

unconscious body was neatly stacked on top of his two guards against the wall. Thousands of pounds of banknotes were spilling from the pockets of the three of them. The safe door was open and inside more stacks of notes were clumsily heaped. Roach whipped out his mobile and took photos, documenting the scene. Ensuring that the less-scrupulous of his colleagues wouldn't go home with a five-finger bonus.

He quickly snapped the pile of unconscious bodies, zoomed in on a couple of the injuries that were immediately obvious. One guy's hand looked particularly nasty. Next he snapped around the room, the bookcase, the fireplace and finally he approached the safe. He snapped away and then one of the notes, caught by some unseen breeze, fluttered out and landed by his foot.

Roach titled his head to one side, looking down at it. And then it struck him. It was the same serial number as the fakes that little shitehawk Lucas had given him. If he wasn't in this up to his neck then Roach would be amazed…

He approach the safe and examined the notes more closely. They all had an identical serial number. Turning around, he caught one of the other officers reaching in to a guard's pocket about to take a handful.

"Fake," he said.

Scarfe took a step forward and was about to say something when the carpet squelched under his shoe. "What the—?"

"There was a woman," said Roach. "I heard a woman's voice. So either she was a victim or she's somehow managed to take out two armed men and our friendly, neighbourhood crime boss. With her bare hands. And then vanished into thin air."

"Could have been speakerphone?" said Scarfe.

Roach shook his head. "Nah, she was definitely here."

He scanned the room, his eyes creeping from nook to cranny. Apart from under the desk, there was nowhere anyone could hide. Elias groaned and Roach walked over to check on him. Scarfe dropped to one knee, inspecting the damp stain on the ground. He dipped his fingers in it and raised them to his mouth, his tongue darting out to taste it, when…

"No!" Roach barked, seeing the damp patch around Elias' crotch.

Scarfe stopped just in time and growled. "Who did this?" he demanded.

The two detectives stalked the room, moving furniture, paintings, looking for hatches, hiding places, perhaps even the possibility of a panic room. The office was big. But not that big.

"Look," Scarfe gestured to the compartment that had contained the Zenka's ashes in the fireplace.

Roach nodded in agreement. Something had been there. Something other than the counterfeit notes. But it was gone. And so was she.

Finally, Roach looked up.

The loft hatch.

He tapped his finger on his partner's shoulder before raising it to his lips, motioning him to silence.

Scarfe's face was still collapsed in an angry frown,

but he did as he was told. Roach pointed up to the hatch.

His partner nodded and, with great difficulty, the two of them dragged the desk so that a corner of it was under the opening. Roach motioned for Scarfe to take the lead, but his partner just sneered at him. Pulling a small flashlight from his coat, Roach hopped up onto the desk.

He took a breath. He didn't know what he would find up there, but judging by the havoc that whoever it was had left behind, they wouldn't be friendly. He reached up and pushed the hatch out of the way.

There was no response, no kickback, no noise of a gun being cocked, and so Roach moved the flashlight to his mouth, gripping it between clenched teeth, and hauled himself up so the top half of his body was in the loft space. The flashlight illuminated a patch of blank wall but nothing else. As quickly as he was able, he hoisted himself further so he was sitting on the edge of the loft hatch and then took the flashlight from his mouth, flicking it around the accumulated detritus. Nothing but Christmas decorations and…

With an almighty bang an explosion cracked through the darkened corners, the shock waves hitting Roach. For a moment, time slowed down. He panicked, his hands grabbing at anything that might be in front of him, looking for purchase and finding nothing but thin air. In an instant he was thrown against the wall and fell back through the hatch, hitting Scarfe and the desk as he dropped back into the room.

"What the fuck is going on?" Scarfe screamed. "What the fuck was that? Are you shot?"

Roach staggered slightly as he got to his feet. "Bomb," was all he could manage to say. As the ringing in his ears subsided, he added, "Next door. She's covering her tracks. She's going to try to escape through the nightclub."

"Or burn to death trying," said Scarfe.

"I'm going after her," replied Roach. "And don't even think about trying to hide the money. I've got photos."

Scarfe raised a long middle finger at Roach. "Careful you don't get killed," he said, unconvincingly.

Roach shrugged and ran for the lift. There was no way he would let this slippery bugger get away.

THIRTEEN

So THIS WAS IT, thought Katie. They were going to die. Well, Violet was going to die. Katie had put her firefighter's uniform on again, replete with mask and breathing apparatus. Violet's outfit was a little lighter on protection from a painful, fiery death.

Katie nudged an empty smoke grenade canister. It had long since stopped spewing smoke, but its emissions still hung in the air, adding a dreamlike quality to the surroundings. There must have been ventilation somewhere, because she could see her hand in front of her face, but it hadn't dispersed the smoke entirely.

There was a huge bang and the door to the manager's office opened and slammed itself. She peered through the glass to the staircase beyond. It didn't look too bad, the fire hadn't reached this floor yet. Katie ran the timeline in her head, calculating how far it might have spread.

Thirty seconds is all it would take to consume the bins, the fire taking easily on the paper and cardboard of the recycling. In the next minute, as the heat increased, paint, wallpaper, and some of the fittings would go up in flames. A dark plume of smoke rose up the middle of the stairwell. That would be hot, too. Hot enough to burn your lungs, if you weren't wearing apparatus. And Violet wasn't. Two, maybe three breaths was all she'd manage, and then their best hope would be to get her resuscitated outside. If the structural integrity of the ancient stairs held.

The heat might not prove to be their biggest problem. Carbon monoxide poisoning would likely get Violet first. But they'd been dealing with Elias for more than a couple of minutes. It had been at least ten minutes, maybe more. There was every chance the fire had reached the stage where there'd be a flashover — everything spontaneously bursting into flames. Violet had used accelerant. Even if the actual firefighters were dowsing it, those stairs were most likely…

Katie reached forward to push open the door and inspect their escape route, but a hand on her right shoulder stopped her. Instinctively, Katie grabbed the hand at the wrist, and twisted it as she turned.

"Fuck's sake, Katie," said Violet, trying to extricate herself from her friend's grip. Katie let go. Violet massaged her wrist in pain, and was about to say something else, but the grenade-smoke filled her lungs and she spluttered.

"Don't… open… that… door…" she managed between coughs. The blood still framed her teeth as she spoke and Katie could see a cut on the side of Violet's forehead, all over her face bruises were blossoming. Her left cheek where Elias' guard had slapped her had puffed out a little and there were several finger marks beginning to bruise too. Her right cheek where the guard had hit her was worse. An open-palm, calculated slap with a hand large enough to reach from her cheek to her rapidly-blackening eye. Violet's bottom lip had taken damage too, it looked split and there was dried blood in the corner of her mouth.

Katie motioned downwards and dropped to a crouch. Violet followed suit, the air marginally clearer at this height. She pointed at the door, but Violet shook her head and pointed to the other end of the corridor. Katie stood up once more as Violet crawled along on her hands and knees. From down there, Violet could only see up to Katie's waist. She tried to make some Jack and the Beanstalk crack, but got another lungful of grenade-smoke and just coughed instead.

They reached the pile of chairs at the end of the corridor and Katie crouched once more. Violet propped herself against the wall. Behind the chairs was a door.

"I don't suppose I could get you to…" Violet coughed and waved at the chairs.

Katie nodded and hurled them down the corridor, each one vanishing into the greyish cloud long before the clatter of it hitting the floor was heard. This was taking too long. They should have left through the office next door, but Violet had insisted they go through the burning building… Katie rattled the handle of the door but it was locked.

Violet rummaged in her bag for lock picks, when another explosion crashed into the corridor. The two women stared into the fog as it changed colour. Orange shadows danced through the light grenade-smoke and then the dark, hot smoke that Katie had seen through the glass began to pour towards them.

"Is it… hot in here…" Violet spluttered, "or… just…"

Katie looked down at her friend, her heartbeat quickening. They didn't have time for this. She turned to the door and kicked it with all her might. It buckled inwards, her strength shattering it. She cleared the remaining splinters with her fire axe to reveal… an old, unused cupboard.

"Ah…" spluttered Violet. "Shit."

Katie cocked her head to one side, waiting for an explanation, to hear where their escape route was. And then she saw it; the walls, the ceiling, the whole corridor wasn't simply alight, it was blazing towards them, the fire spitting its orange hatred down the corridor like a dragon's belch.

She looked back down at Violet.

"That was supposed to be a staircase," Violet managed before the hacking coughs took her, wracking her body until she lay, gasping for breath, flat on the floor.

Katie suddenly felt a great deal less calm. It wasn't just Violet who would die in that corridor.

FOURTEEN

ROACH HIT THE PAVEMENT RUNNING.

He'd been running since he left Elias' office. The lifts that had been so accommodating earlier had shut off when some bright spark had finally realised the fire had spread to the office from the nightclub. He was fit, he was fast, but as he tore down flight after flight of stairs he'd been increasingly frustrated at the time he had to apprehend the escapees ebbing away.

He skidded to a halt as he reached the crowds. The police cordon was still in place, but the revellers were now twenty deep. Word must have travelled on social media and waves of inebriated idiots had flocked to watch the Palace burn. Roach squeezed through the mob, moving steadily towards the entrance to the burning club. It wasn't just punters, he noticed. An opportunistic fast-food entrepreneur had set up a van and was selling greasy kebabs and burgers to anyone who wanted them. It was difficult to see where the fast-food queue ended and the crowd of rubber-necked gawkers began. Perhaps they were all in the queue.

"Detective." One of the uniforms recognised him and lifted the tape, holding back some alpha-arsehole who thought he might chance his luck to get through at the same time.

"Radio everyone," said Roach, his breathing returning to normal. "If anyone comes out of the club I want them held for questioning. Understand?"

The uniform acknowledged him and Roach nodded his thanks. He stared at the Palace. Windows he had never noticed before were spewing fire, the wind pushing the flames towards Elias' beautiful glass office. Inside the club would be worse. If the fire had taken that side of the building the suspect would probably be lost. So not all bad then, he thought, allowing himself a smirk before a voice behind him invaded his ruminations.

"…puked all over me. I think she might still be in there, passed out in the lavs, but no-one will listen."

Roach turned around to see a woman who looked like she'd had a significantly worse night than he had so far. She wore what looked like expensive shoes, the sort his ex-girlfriend had called 'sitting down shoes' but, at a second glance they were obvious fakes. She didn't wear a coat and her red silk dress was blotched with an unknown fluid. Looking more closely at the splash pattern confirmed that the vomit was from a third party. This was backed up by the fact that she also had little chunks of it nestling in her otherwise perfectly styled beehive hairdo.

Roach showed her his warrant card. "Miss?" he said, commanding her attention. "Would you like to explain what happened?"

Beehive fluttered her false eyelashes at him. "Constable," she smiled.

Roach was about to correct her but the urgency of the situation got the better of him. "Miss…" he encouraged.

"I work in the club as a restroom attendant and…"

"I'm sure you can see how busy we are, Miss," Roach rushed her as his brain fought between getting the story out of a potential witness and catching his quarry in the act. "If you can tell me just the pertinent facts as quickly as you can. Where did it happen?"

"A woman was sick on me," she said.

"And whilst I have every sympathy, I'm not yet seeing the relevance. It happened—"

"In the toilets," she interrupted, pointing at the Palace.

"When?"

"A couple of seconds before the alarms started—"

Roach interrupted right back. "Where are the toilets exactly."

The woman told him. "She went into a cubicle. I think she might still be there. I mean, what a bitch, right? But I don't want her to die."

Something wasn't right. There was something off about all of this and he couldn't quite see what it was. Roach stared at the woman for a moment, taking it all in again, the matted hair, the dress, the shoes. The smell. There was no smell. He leaned forward and sniffed.

Beehive instinctively recoiled and tried to step away but the crowd behind her meant there was nowhere for her to go.

"That's not vomit," he said.

"What?"

Roach reached forward and, despite her cries of protest, he touched her hair, bringing some of the supposed-sick to his nose. He sniffed it, lightly at first, then with a great, heaving intake through his nose.

Beehive dry-heaved as he did.

"Definitely not vomit."

"But it came out of her mouth! She was absolutely hammered." Beehive's face was a mask of disgust. "It's all over me."

"Could you give me a description of her?"

"What?" asked Beehive, apparently unable or at least unwilling to understand anything on the first asking.

"A description," said Roach testily. "What did she look like?"

"Oh," she curled her lip. "I dunno. Little taller than me. Black bobbed hair. Sort of athletic build but not skinny-skinny, if you know what I mean."

Roach nodded. So this was who had escaped from the office. A woman. How the hell she'd flattened three seasoned hardcases was another story entirely but one he was very much looking forward to getting out of her. He beckoned to the uniformed officer he'd just spoken to. "We'll need a statement from her. I think she may prove relevant."

Uniform shrugged and lifted the tape, allowing

Beehive access to their side whilst Roach moved off to find the nearest firefighter.

"What's your name?" Roach asked, a warm smile on his face.

The firefighter was tall and looked like he packed out every inch of his uniform. His black hair was severely cut and matched the bags under his eyes. "Steve," he said.

Roach's face instantly dropped back into seriousness. "You need to take me inside, Steve."

Steve the firefighter remained distinctly underwhelmed.

"Nah, mate." His voice was deep and hoarse. "Too dangerous for you in there."

Roach nodded, walked past him and quickly broke into a jog as he headed for the doors.

"Oi, come back, you wanker!" Steve shouted after him. Instead of stopping, Roach ran faster. The firefighter cursed under his breath and grabbed his helmet before giving chase.

Roach was by the cloakroom when the firefighter caught up with him.

Smoke hung in the air, but like the vomit, it smelled... *wrong*.

"Does this look like a proper fire to you?" Roach asked.

Steve squinted at him. "Are you fucking high?"

Roach paused, not sure if he was dealing with an idiot. "The smoke. It smells wrong."

The penny dropped. "Right, yeah. Reckon it's a

smoke grenade. Someone trying to keep us out while the fire takes."

"So it's arson?"

Steve nodded. "Most likely."

"Do you know where the ladies are?" Roach asked.

"Erm," the firefighter replied in confusion. "What ladies?"

"No... I mean... Never mind." Roach spotted the sign for the ladies toilets through the smoke and bounded off towards it, with the firefighter in close pursuit. "There's someone in there. The toilet attendant thinks she might be trapped." It wasn't a complete lie but the truth was a scent barely sniffable against the stench of obfuscation.

The foyer to the club was soaked from the firefighters' hoses. Roach ground his teeth at the thought of all that lost forensics, but was soon distracted by the sight of the fire, which was well and truly established off in the direction of the dance floor. It was no wonder Elias' building had caught — the fire seemed to be worst on the adjoining side of the building.

Roach pushed at the door to the toilets and it gave easily. There was no smoke in there, so he stepped inside. Even in the midst of the building collapsing with the fire, and without proper lighting, it never ceased to amaze him how much nicer women's toilets were than the men's.

Steve propped the door open with his shoulder. "Seriously, mate," he said, "you've got two minutes. One hundred and twenty seconds and then I'm taking you out of here. Over my shoulder if I have to."

Roach felt the urge to challenge him. Pushed down the words *'you can try'*. He made eye contact with the firefighter in the big mirror that ran along the wall behind the sinks and nodded.

Beehive's description of what had happened held up in here, too. The trajectory and spatter of the vomit — or whatever it was — was as she described it.

"Hello?" he shouted. "Anyone in here?" He didn't expect an answer but better not burst into cubicles without fair warning. "This is the police and fire service. We're here to rescue you."

Silence.

The detective went to the cubicle nearest the exit and pushed open its door. Empty.

He stepped left and pushed the next one open. Empty.

And another. And another. And another. All empty.

He could feel the firefighter's impatience but ignored it as he nudged the last cubicle door open and found…

Nothing.

He let the door swing shut and turned away, but something in the back of his brain told him to wait. He opened it again and stepped inside the stall. There, behind the toilet, down by the bleach and the brush were a pair of shoes. He picked them up, his eyes quickly scanning the small cubicle until… a skirt and a top shoved behind the cistern. He grabbed them and put the garments into his coat pocket, holding on to the shoes by the heels like the campest gunfighter in the north.

"Right," he said, walking out past the firefighter. "Just need to check the dance floor and…"

"Oh no," Steve protested once more. "The fire's properly taken in there. There's no way…"

Roach sprinted towards the flames, damned if he would let them get away, but the heat hit him like a belly flop from an angry bear and he staggered to a halt. Squinting at the orange glare, he spluttered with the smoke and could feel the burn from the air in the back of his throat. At first glance, it looked like the fire was concentrated at the bar and was being reflected in the mirrored ceiling tiles. Until he realised that the ceiling wasn't mirrored. It was just burning.

The detective felt a hand on his shoulder. As he turned around to placate his pursuer, a pair of doors at the end of the bar exploded.

A plume of flames attacked the dance floor, and the back draft smashed into Roach and the firefighter, hurling them backwards and into unconsciousness.

FIFTEEN

"KATIE," spluttered Violet, her voice hoarse. She clung to the floor as if it were a sheer rock face. "We need to make an exit. Now."

Katie shifted uncomfortably. If she didn't share the breathing apparatus Violet was going to die. If she did then there was every chance they both would.

"In there." Violet pointed to the cupboard.

Katie cocked her head to one side.

Violet kicked the head of the axe that hung by Katie's side. "MAKE an exit. Now."

Violet convulsed, her whole body wracked with a fit of coughing. Katie didn't hesitate. She launched herself at the cupboard, hefting the axe at its back wall. She expected to hit brick but instead the axe ploughed through the plasterboard. She twisted the head of the great, heavy beast and pulled it back towards her.

A black hole the size of a head was left behind.

Katie swung again and again and again until a constellation of holes dotted the back of the cupboard.

Then she took a few steps back and ran, throwing the whole of her six foot ten inch frame at it. The old plasterboard gave way completely and she tumbled into the void beyond.

A moment later and the darkness shrank away as Katie turned on her flashlight. She was on a landing. There were stairs. They were old and rotten and they could barely take her weight but they were stairs and, as far as she could see, they were not on fire. Not yet. No plumes of smoke, just dusty darkness and cobwebs. Cobwebs she could deal with.

She moved fast, striding back to Violet and scooping her up and over her shoulder. Anyone else might have been weighed down by carrying another human on their back but for Katie it barely seemed to register. The landing floorboards creaked in complaint at their combined weight but they would hold for long enough. There was a beauty in her agility. A terrifying efficiency with not even a centimetre of wasted movement as she descended floor by floor, the stairs spiralling down and down into the darkness. As fast as she moved, there was never a moment when Violet's hanging head or other extremities were in any danger of swinging to hit against a wall or dusty finial.

Footsteps clattering with a muffled echo, Katie made short work of the descent, gently lowering Violet down to sit on the bottom few steps. She gave her friend's shoulder a little squeeze. Her breathing was laboured, but she was conscious. There was a door at the bottom of the stairs, panelled and with peeling white paint.

Katie tried the handle and, to her great surprise, it turned.

It came as no surprise whatsoever that behind the door was a crudely constructed brick wall. She tested it with her foot. It was too strong to just kick out but…

Using the flat of the head of the fire axe, Katie attacked the left side of the brickwork. Strike after strike sent brick dust into the air until one brick came loose. Katie reached over and plucked it out, tossing it to one side then hooked the axe into the gap and yanked.

She had to hop backwards to stop the avalanche of bricks from crushing her. The wall was down and it revealed…

Another wall.

Katie clenched her fists around the fire axe. She'd had just about enough of this shit.

SIXTEEN

A SINGLE LIGHTING rig still danced on in the face of the defeat of all its brothers and sisters at the hands of the fire. The Tulip Street Gin Palace was being treated to the best, most immersive, three dimensional light and sound show known to man. Known to every man since the first man got a bit too handy with two sticks and accidentally set fire to his cave.

The fire behind the bar was bleeding into the building, spraying flames upwards like a severed artery. The dropped ceiling was ablaze above the dance floor, which, at that moment, had a detective with what appeared to be a death wish running across it. He was reluctantly followed by a firefighter who looked like, at any moment, he might just hit the detective over the head with something heavy and drag him out of there.

Perhaps sensing the impending loss of life, the firefighter put on a burst of speed, reaching the detective and putting his hand on his shoulder. But it was too late. The doors at the end of the bar exploded, throwing the detective into the firefighter, knocking them like skittles to the edge of the dance floor.

After the aural abuse of the explosion, a quiet calm descended. The kind of background noise you might expect on a beach, but instead of the tides washing in and out, it was the contented roar of the fire devouring the building. Through the calm came a tapping.

You might have heard it if you had been standing in the middle of the dance floor. If it was midday on a Tuesday and the music wasn't playing. And if the building wasn't on the verge of collapse.

If you'd turned around, away from the bar, you might have noticed a movement on the opposite wall. Behind one booth, something was happening. The light glinted off an object that wasn't there a moment earlier. And then it was gone. The object returned, this time in a tiny puff of masonry dust and the light glinted off it once more. Finally the head of an axe was picked out in the dying disco lights before the whole of the lighting rig finally gave up the ghost and the club collapsed into darkness.

The plaster of the wall burst open. In the hole that remained stood Katie, resplendent in her firefighter uniform, torch flicking around, hoping, praying, that this time there wouldn't be another damn wall in the way. She disappeared for a moment before returning with Violet over her shoulder. This was it. The final stretch.

She stepped through the hole she'd created, knocking over glasses as she clambered over the table top. She could see the foyer, the doors. This was it.

Katie picked up speed, desperate now to get away

from the flames, but as she reached the far edge of the dance floor she saw them. Two bodies lying prone on the ground. For a moment she didn't waver, just kept going for the door, but a few steps later she stopped, lowering Violet to the ground.

Violet propped herself against the wall.

"Wha…?" was all she managed through the coughing.

Katie gestured towards the men and Violet hesitated for a moment before nodding.

Katie hadn't been asking permission, but that was beside the point. She moved quickly, hooking her arms under the armpits of the man who wasn't a firefighter. She dragged him away from the danger zone, his heels scraping along the floor. His head twitched as consciousness leaked back into him.

She strode back to the dancefloor and repeated the process for the firefighter in his matching yellow uniform.

The non-firefighter had propped himself up on the soaked carpet. He tried to say something but it just came out as a croak.

Katie nodded her response and waved towards the fire as a warning. He blinked sore eyes at her and nodded back.

Now that those two were safe… escape. Violet was still coughing as Katie scooped her up and over her shoulder one last time. Striding forward, she shoved open the doors. She stood for a moment, grateful for the cold night air, even through all the layers of protection she wore.

Roach's consciousness was returning like an adulterous girlfriend trying to sneak into the house unnoticed at 4:30 a.m., still so inebriated that she falls down the stairs three times on the walk of shame back to the bedroom. His senses seemed to be drifting back to him as though they were all being rebooted at different speeds.

Until his rescuer opened the door.

There was a rush of cold air and in an instant all his senses came back online. He sat bolt upright. He could instantly feel the damp seeping into the arse of his trousers. It would look like he'd pissed himself when he stood up.

He'd been dragged to safety. The adrenal swell of frustration rose inside him as he stared at his rescuer about to leave. Roach got to his feet and immediately regretted it, a woozy feeling flooding his body like a waterfall from his brain.

His rescuer had scooped up another casualty and was carrying her outside, her dark bobbed hair flopping loosely and obscuring her features.

Her black bobbed hair.

It was her. The suspect.

Katie ducked her head to fit through the door and Roach suddenly knew how the tiny woman with the bobbed hair had taken down three people whose primary purpose in life was to fuck other people up. She had a... a... giant on the payroll.

Roach turned to make sure Steve was moving in an 'out' direction then ran for Katie, trying to shout, the smoke still stuck in his throat turning his words into hisses.

Katie was already en route into the crowd and to Barry's recently acquired ambulance, parked exactly where he'd promised it would be. Seeing that she was carrying an apparently injured member of the public, even the other emergency services scuttled out of Katie's way, allowing her to get away from the Palace unhindered.

Violet raised her head far enough to see the results of her handiwork. The fire wasn't just pouring out of the first floor windows. The whole of the nightclub was ablaze, with the majority of the adjoining side of Elias' office up in flames too. She smiled and let her head drop into the small of Katie's back once more.

SEVENTEEN

DETECTIVE ROACH's thoughts were like quicksilver now. How could he have missed the fact that the suspect had an accomplice? He squelched forward in pursuit but found himself pausing for a beat by the cloakroom, his mind circling back to that woman. The woman with the dark bobbed hair.

More than one woman in the world had dark bobbed hair. It could be someone else. What evidence did he have that she was the woman the toilet attendant had seen? The same woman who had got changed in the cubicle and left behind... The clothes. Where were the clothes? The adrenaline was surging through his system and he spun around, looking for the clothes he had rescued from the toilet cubicle. He must have dropped them on the dance floor. They would be burned to a crisp by now, except — No, one shoe was on the stair next to where the firefighter had dragged him.

He sprinted back for it and then turned and ran for the door. She was definitely the woman. He could feel it in his gut. Skidding to a halt outside the club, he surveyed the scene, her shoe held tight in his fist like he was a justice-seeking Prince Charming. She wasn't hard to spot. The firefighter carrying her was taller than everyone else in the crowd. And the woman's backpack poked into the air like a hunchback as she hung over the firefighter's shoulder.

A backpack. Who takes a backpack to a nightclub? No-one, that's who. Roach surged towards them, but a cadre of yellow-uniformed firefighters ran in his way, dragging hoses in their wake. The tall firefighter had lowered his quarry into the back of the ambulance and taken off his helmet. Not his helmet. *Her* helmet. It was a woman. A giant woman.

For a moment Roach had to have a word with himself, tell himself that this was not the raving of a man who had just had a near-death experience. What he was seeing was very real indeed. The giantess threw her helmet to the ground before discarding her jacket in the same way and folding herself into the back of the ambulance.

Roach shoved his way through the crowd, wrenching drunks and kebab-munchers out of his way, but it was like running through a swimming pool of inebriated custard.

The blue ambulance lights flickered to life and the crowds parted as the vehicle pulled away. Finally catching up with the ambulance, Roach banged on the driver's window. The driver turned to look at him with a shit-eating grin. It was the helpful paramedic from Elias

Croft's reception area, which could only mean one thing. Roach had been played from start to finish.

He pulled at the locked door of the ambulance, but as the vehicle reached the edge of the crowd Barry switched on the siren. Roach jumped at the sudden ear-splitting din but kept his eyes on the driver. Once Barry was sure he wasn't about to flatten a piss-head, he turned back to Roach and saluted him before lowering his hand and curling back all but his middle finger. He gave the tip of the raised digit a little kiss and, accelerating through the red lights at an intersection, drove off into the night.

"FUCK!" Roach screamed after them. The words echoed back from darkened buildings that towered around him, doing nothing to assuage his rage. The bastards had got away with whatever the hell they had stolen and all Roach had to show for it was one lady's shoe.

But there would be a next time. There was always a next time.

He turned around to see a television crew approaching the reception of Elias' building just as the man himself was being led towards the main door, hands neatly and unavoidably cuffed behind his back.

Roach let out a little sigh that could possibly have been construed as relief. If it could be said that he had bigger fish to fry then this fish had just been delivered to him, freshly caught and with an enormous hook through its ugly face.

Elias wasn't going to be able to buy his way out of this one and, more importantly, the evidence was overwhelming enough that no-one would help him. Not Scarfe, not anyone.

The blue light from the ambulance disappeared from view and Roach strode purposefully toward Elias Croft, ex-gangster.

EIGHTEEN

THE SHUTTERS of the garage cut them off from the outside world. Barry turned off the ambulance headlights and, for a moment, there was nothing but darkness.

Then light spilled onto the concrete floor as the door to the inside of the house opened and first Lucas, then Zoe stepped out to greet them. Lucas fumbled around the wall next to the door, finally flicking a switch and causing the neon tubes above them to stutter to life.

Barry threw open the driver's door and jumped down, his feet slapping on the ground and echoing around the bare walls.

Lucas and Zoe shared the same wide-eyed, expectant look.

"Well?" asked Lucas.

Barry grinned and pointed his thumb to the back of the ambulance. "They're both in the back and so are the ashes. Got any beer?"

Lucas grabbed Barry by the hand and pumped it up

and down. "You bloody legends," he said. "In the fridge. We waited."

"And the building?" asked Zoe.

"Both torched," said Barry over his shoulder as he stepped past them and disappeared into the house. "Might be on the news."

"The news?" said Lucas gleefully, turning to follow Barry.

"What about Violet and Katie?" Zoe asked, but before she could pursue the line of questioning any further there was a *clunk* as the back doors of the ambulance were thrown open.

Zoe darted around excitedly to hear the blow by blow account straight from Violet's mouth but stopped short, her lips frozen in an 'o' shape at what she saw.

Violet was lying on a stretcher in the back of the ambulance. Her face was a patchwork of welts and bruises, the blood that had been running over it and into her hair caked dry from the heat of the fire.

Katie carefully took the oxygen mask from her mouth and revealed more; the fat, burst lip, more deep, purple bruises.

"Jesus fucking Christ, is she alive?" Zoe managed.

The smell of smoke was becoming increasingly noticeable with every passing second.

Katie looked at Violet, then at Zoe and, for a second, Zoe thought Katie might shake her head in the negative.

Then Violet sat bolt upright and coughed. Big, hacking, full-lung coughs that sandpapered her throat on the way out.

Zoe breathed out but continued looking at Katie for an answer. Katie raised her eyebrows, tilted her head to one side and held out her thumb and forefinger about an inch apart.

"Never… mind… that…" Violet managed between coughs.

Katie shook her head and swung the bag towards Zoe, who caught it and hugged it tight to her chest.

"We got a bite online. A buyer," said Zoe, trying to distract, but her eyes remained fixed on Violet as Katie helped her to her feet.

Violet nodded and smiled. The smile only worked on one side, the other immobile from the swelling.

Lucas leaned through the door from the house, can of lager in hand. "You should see what's on the telly," he said, before noticing the state of Violet. "Do you need a hand?"

"She's fine." Barry's voice was muffled from inside the house. "Doesn't need any help. Hard as nails is Violet."

Lucas raised a dubious eyebrow. "I know you said it would be risky but I thought you meant, you know… police risky. Incarceration risky. Not… Fubar risky."

Zoe squinted at him in confusion. "Old man reference?" she asked.

Lucas clicked his teeth irritatedly. "I'm not old."

"You are to me," said Zoe, handing him the backpack. "Take this inside."

Lucas took it and Zoe went over to Violet, letting her lean lightly on her shoulder as she walked slowly inside.

Katie moved off but stopped in the doorway when Violet spoke. "Katie," she said, her voice as dry as sand.

Katie didn't turn.

"Are we… okay?" Violet asked.

Katie turned her head, her powerful jawline picked out and backlit. She seemed to deflate slightly but she nodded just once.

"Some risks aren't worth taking, you know," said Zoe as they stepped inside. "We didn't need to—"

"Reputation is everything," said Violet, simply.

Zoe understood. She didn't like it but there was no denying that this was a massive fuck you to anyone who dared cross them and a huge, skyscraper-sized hoarding advertising their services and talents.

The living room of the house they'd rented was so large they could have comfortably hosted a gig from a mid-level indie band, the television that hung on the longest wall so big it could have been mistaken for a cinema screen.

"…scenes tonight at the Tulip Street Gin Palace," said the announcer on the news. She gripped her microphone and tried to rise above the drunken rabble hell-bent on exhibiting the sort of behaviour that would undoubtedly go viral online the following day. "The blaze took hold earlier this evening and quickly spread to the offices of notorious *businessman* Elias Croft. Miraculously there seem to have been no deaths and, so far, we've only seen one ambulance leaving the scene so casualties are expected to be in single figures."

Barry reached down by his chair and, without warning, sent a bottle spinning through the air across the room. Katie caught it mid-air, inspected it, then uncorked it and took a pull. "I got the good stuff for you," he said.

Katie nodded in appreciation and flopped backwards onto the sofa, taking up all of the room without bothering to spread out.

"Also I'm hearing," the newsreader pushed her earpiece deeper to drown out the drunks. "I'm hearing that we've received footage... in the studio... security footage... proving that Mr Croft set the fire himself."

"Was that us?" asked Barry.

"Of course it bloody was," said Lucas, sipping at his beer. "Zoe set it up and I knocked it out of the park."

"Don't forget to give me that phone," said Zoe.

Violet said something but Zoe didn't catch it over the newsreader. She leaned in closer and Violet managed one word: *bathroom*.

"Just leave her, Zoe," said Barry, his eyes fixed on the TV. "She's just looking for attention."

Katie scowled and Barry shut up.

In the bathroom Violet dropped to her knees and gripped the bowl.

"Go," she said.

Zoe ignored her. "No, this is on all of us," she said, holding back Violet's hair.

"And it appears that Elias Croft is being escorted from his own building by the police." The newsreader could barely disguise the glee in her voice. This was her BAFTA, the perfect shot of the gangster being taken into custody while his nightclub and his office burn behind him.

Barry turned the TV up to drown out the sounds of Violet retching.

"Once a pillar of the community," the newsreader padded. "Recently accusations of bribery have surfaced and there has even been suggestion of involvement in organised crime." Her face said *we all know he's guilty*. "And what's this?" she said, as she intercepted Elias before he could reach the police van. "Mr Croft appears to have soiled himself. Have you soiled yourself, Mr Croft?" She thrust the microphone under his nose.

Elias Croft was done. Done with organised crime. Done with his business. Done with being a free man. Now he was a penniless ex-gangster standing in the street on national television having recently pissed himself.

He declined to comment.

"I can confirm that Elias Croft *has indeed* soiled himself and is being led away by the police." If this was going to be her BAFTA she would make the most of it. "Officer? Will you be charging Mr Croft?"

Roach nodded. He managed not to grin but there was a smirk forming at the edges of his mouth. "Nothing's happening until he's been cleaned up," he said.

"This is Sally Fowler for BBC News at the Tulip Street Gin Palace, Kilchester handing back to you in the studio, Mike."

ACKNOWLEDGMENTS

It may be my name on the cover but prising Kilchester diamonds from the word mines is most certainly a group activity.

Firstly to my wife Eve whose importance required that her thanks were in a larger font than everyone else. Thank you for putting up with my obsession with Violet and the gang and for being the finest muse to have existed down the ages.

To my daughter Nina - what the hell are you doing reading this? You're twelve years old. Swearing isn't funny OR cool. Don't use Violet as a role model. And if you do, don't get caught.

James Whitman, my co-conspirator and now editor. Thank you for never saying 'well, that sounds like a fucking stupid idea' whilst still ensuring that any fucking stupid ideas don't get through. And for championing the very fucking stupidest and helping me elevate them beyond their worth. Your input is absolutely invaluable.

To the gents from the Story Toolkit podcast. Literally every author should listen to their incisive ramblings if they want to level up. Luke Lyon-Wall - your email encouragement is appreciated enormously. The impact your insight has on writers of all abilities is not to be underestimated. And to your co-rambler Bassim El-Wakil…

I sent Bass the original outline for this book and his insight into the characters and advice on how to improve the book as a whole was frankly more than a little scary. Your ability to cut through the shit and identify what was and wasn't working was so accurate that at some point I'm certain you'll be burned as a witch. Until then I can only hope the changes I made did the trick.

My co-editors Elaine Jinks-Turner and Sam Hartburn have the eagle-eyed accuracy of… well… eagles. Thank you for your eyes and minds. I would be fearful to publish without your assistance.

Mister Matthew Austin. Even by moving to Australia you cannot escape the pull of Kilchester. To the last I was tweaking the manuscript to your advice. And including jokes that only you will get.

Michael Brett, thank you for listening to me banging on about Kilchester every bloody time we meet up.

Thanks to my experts… Dean Coulson for making me less fat and for being a brilliant fight co-ordinator and helping Katie be what she is. A goddess. But a goddamn dangerous one. Carlos Echevarria for his insight into medical procedures and David Kelly for not reporting me to the police when I asked him how to make sausages out of human flesh. Tony Hutchinson for his insight and advice in terms of police procedure.

Once again the cover illustration by Mute. People judge a book by its cover and I couldn't be happier by them judging me by your immense talent.

To Fergus McNeill for being not just a great writer but generous enough with his time to read my novella. I couldn't be prouder of the blurb you wrote. Fingers crossed it'll help convince people to take a punt on the book but more than that I'm over the moon you liked it as much as you did. The next pint is on me.

Thanks to my advance readers, especially Brenda West for your unrivalled insights!

Paul Jones and Garry Willey from Cheshire Cat Books - thank you for your help from the shadows and going forward.

Lastly, but most certainly not leastly thank you to the Kilchester Irregulars. I know I sent you gifts but it was only because I love you all.

- A.M.

Printed in Great Britain
by Amazon

74891428R00090